I thoroughly enjoyed developing the character of David Death, and hope, if others enjoy him as much as I do, to write more books in the David Death series. A few important notes:

DAVID LIGHT: This is my first book of fiction. David is an opinionated man. (As is the author.) To develop the character there were times I went into a little more detail than many of you would wish to wade through. So, I cut those parts out. But, as some of his rants are crucial to expanding his character, I have included them at the back of the book, rather than the main body. That way, if you prefer **'David light'** you just keep reading. For more detail as to what he believes and why, flip to the page indicated Similarly, because David finds himself in conflict with a vicious biker gang, a more detailed discussion of such things as biker gang lore and history can be found in the back. If you have no interest in such things, just keep reading. If your interest is piqued, go to page indicated. Finally, in the same vein, their are sections in the back that contain some of David's recipes, examples of David's writing under his pen name, Damion's jokes etc. These are included as a bonus, and also to gauge interest for upcoming books I have planned. Information can be found on how to obtain copies and/or contribute at www.barrytuddenham.com.

It should be noted that all the characters are fictional with the exception of Tish and Jodie of the charity Cats Anonymous. These are a couple that I admire greatly. They play a very minor role in this book, the first of what I hope to be a series of David death books. What I say about them and their charity is real. If you like what you hear about them, they could surely do with your support. More information on them can be found at www.catsanonymous.ca , and info in some exceptional give a ways and contests you can enter can be found on www.barrytuddenham.com . I promise you, you will find a visit there worthwhile!

I would like to thank my mother. First for having me...I would not be here without her :-) Second for putting up with me...I was a hand-full growing up. Third for taking the time to correct my more outrageous punctuation mistakes. At 96, her mind is still as sharp as it ever was.

Enjoy!

Barry Tuddenham.

THE EVIL ONES.

We all have our own brand of crazy . We all hide dark secrets. Some hide better than others. Some hide more than others. None of us is perfect, yet we all like to judge others. I ask you not to judge me too harshly until I have had a chance to explain.

There is an old adage that says cream rises to the top. It is supposed to explain why the best succeed .. in business, in politics, in just about any human endeavour. What the adage forgets is that scum rises to the top of cream.... a very, very thin layer over the cream....but it is there . In business, in politics, in just about any human endeavour. The very top of that scum on the cream is often inhabited by psychopaths. Very very smart psychopaths.

Then there are groups like the gang known as The Evil Ones. Not much cream there. Quite a lot of scum.

I propose a new adage: The worse scum always rises to the top.

I have known lots of very smart people that for some reason or another never made it to the top. Conversely, I have known real idiots that somehow did. That kind of gives the lie to that old adage. Personally, I have never known an exception to the new one. Unless someone steps in and takes them out.

CHAPTER 1

Here was Smith smiling upon us, his new charges. At 20, he was our camp supervisor, his summer job while home from University. His smile almost made his eyes, but not quite. Would fool most people into thinking he was a friendly guy. I would have known what Smith was, even if Johnny had not warned me. "One mean motherfucker" as Johnny said. I have met far too many psychopaths in my life. Each time I've met one they send an indescribable chill through my body. Smith was the first time I felt that chill. I have since found out that feeling I get is never wrong.

These are pretty much the words Johnny spoke the first time I saw Smith:

"See that guy over there? That's Glenn Smith. May look like the Pillsbury Dough Boy, and Smith may be a common name, but *that* Smith is far from common. A real mean son of a bitch. Watch out for him. My sister tells me he likes to hurt girls, and rumour has it he's the one responsible for all the dog and cat disappearances and mutilations that have been happening lately. Cops even brought him in once when a 15 year old girl disappeared. He was a 'person of interest' to them. They never did find her, and they never could prove their case. My older brother said anyone that fights with him, is going to regret it. Guys that fight him always win fast. Smith folds to stop being hurt too much. But the other guy always gets hurt in the long run far,far worse. They always meet with some kind of a mishap. Don't let that ready smile of his fool you. One mean son of a bitch."

Johnny was one of the guys I had met through the high school gang I hung out with. We were not friends, but he respected me, having seen me fight. Johnny was the toughest and meanest of a tough bunch, so for him to say Smith was a mean son of a bitch meant something. Now, here he was in charge of a summer camp.

"OK kids, we're here to have fun! Welcome to Whispering Pines!" He smiled at each one of us in turn. "Sort yourself out a bunk, and then take a while to look around. Lovely place here. Lovely place. I'll meet you in front of the mess hall right after lunch and we can sort out what activities everyone wants to join in." Once more that beaming smile, then he turned around and left us to sort ourselves out.

Smith had it right. It was a lovely place. As a boy that grew up on the dirty streets of a mining town, a boy that loved nature as if he was born to live in the wild, this was paradise. Well, if it was not paradise, it was a reasonable facsimile thereof, and more beautiful than anything I had known in my 14 years on this earth to that date. I ignored the playing fields the games rooms, the river used by the camp and everyone with a cottage for speed boats and water skiing. I headed into the woods. Blue Jays squawked, squeaked, rattled and whispered amongst themselves , an incredible cacophony of sounds communicating my presence in a complex language that we are too dumb to understand. Crows also sounded the alarm. Swear sometimes it seems crows are smarter than humans. If they had opposing thumbs and a written language they just might rule the world. Chickadees flitted down and I am sure would have landed on my hand if I had had anything worth eating. Love chickadees. Like most little guys, more balls than brains. But, you gotta love em, Other birds and small animals could just be heard making small rustlings, as they moved to let the intruder pass, hoping to go unnoticed. Behind it all, the wind whispered to me as it passed through the trees , told me this was a special place. I was in heaven.

I discovered a pond rich with bulrushes and waterlilies. Sunning on a log about 50 feet off shore were about a dozen painted turtles. They slipped into the water as I approached the shore, creeping back onto the log about ten minutes later, when they figured out I was no threat. Hundreds of minnows scurried away as my shadow past over them. Not so cautious were the bullfrogs. There were a number of dead bullfrogs scattered along the shore, curiously uneaten. Unusual for a predator to kill in such excess and leave the victims to rot. Some of those discarded carcases were huge. The bullfrogs on the lily pads eyed me warily with reptilian, but somehow gentle eyes, and made no move to hide. Every once in a while you would see one swallow. You never really get to see it, but when an insect comes too close, there is a flash of movement, the tongue shoots out, catches the fly and has it back in the frogs mouth before the fly knows it was called to lunch. All you really see is the contented flickering of those huge eyes, and a satisfied swallow.

Darting across the surface of the water, their legs bunched together as they gathered up insects on the fly were at least a dozen different kinds of dragonflies. Effective hunters, they capture dozens of mosquitoes, sometimes up to a hundred a day...and they do it all on the fly, using their legs as a net. Below the surface their young, known as nymphs, are perhaps even more voracious than the flying adults, and eat anything that swims by them, anything that will fit in their mouth, even small fish. Indeed, they take their mouth to the prey, actually thrusting out their lower lip to capture the unwary on hooks located there, just for that purpose, and shooting water out of their rear end to propel them towards their victim. Talk about 'pissing' your victim off!

I find all wildlife fascinating. Indeed, as I've gotten older I began writing stories, even books on what I observed. I write under the name Barry Tuddenham, a name I made up. Was going to use the name Alex Paige-Turner because all the book reviewers seem to use the term "A page turner" to describe the books they are trying to get you to buy .... I figured who the hell wants to read about the exciting life of animals written by a guy named Death?But, Alex Paige-Turner was too much of a joke, taking the pendulum too far the other way. Would not be taken seriously. Besides, most people do not find books on wildlife that exciting. Figured Barry Tuddenham was nice and nondescript. My books are not huge sellers, but I have fun writing them. You can find them if you search hard enough.

Oops, I digress!

I never made it back for lunch that day. Never did get to have Smith assign me to the structured activities he had planned. Although he smiled when he told me I had been left out, I could tell he was pissed off. Here was a man that liked control. I did not give a shit. He called me DeeDee as he spoke to me, instinctively knowing how much it would annoy me. I never gave him the satisfaction of reacting, knowing that if I smashed his face in, my days at camp were over.

(For a sample of David writing as Barry Tuddenham, please see page: 220)

CHAPTER 2

For the next four days, I spent most of my time at the pond, getting to know all the residents, thinking of them as friends. I found that if you picked a long piece of grass with a tassel on the end, you could tickle the bull frogs on the nose and get a reaction. They would get pissed off .... I figure they thought it was an insect showing disrespect. Suddenly they would lunge for the tassel, and clamp on with their huge jaws and short front legs. No simple tongue job for such an annoyance. It was a few feet down from the bank,to where the closest ones took up their positions, but those guys would hang on tight as I hauled them up towards me. They would not let go until they found themselves in my hand. Looking back on it, guess it was kind of mean to tease them like that. But, I was just a kid having fun.

I never meant them any harm. They seemed to realize that, hopping back down the bank and taking back their position on the same lily pad, staring disapprovingly at me with those huge eyes as they clambered back on their pad.

In the evenings, I was up to my usual tricks, winning at arm wrestling, and `teaching` the other kids poker. I took it easy on them, but I was amassing quite a stash of dimes and quarters. A barracks shared with a dozen other guys,is no place to leave valuables,so in the evenings, I would roll up the coins,sleep on top of them, and the next day take them to a secret hiding place out by 'my' pond.

Then it was Sunday. Smith's day off. We were supposed to go to church in the morning, then amuse ourselves at our various activities. I stuffed the rolls of coins from my Saturday night winnings into my pockets, skipped church, and headed for the pond.

As I got close, I could hear chuckling. I was not alone. Creeping quietly up through the bushes, I saw Smith in 'my' spot. Obviously he did not bother with church either. He had a net on a long pole, and was hauling in the bull frog he had just netted, chuckling to himself as he did so. Obviously he did not know the trick with a tasselled grass. But to my horror he showed me a trick with a hollow stemmed piece of grass that only a sick psycho could have dreamed up. I witnessed an unspeakable horror that I still remember vividly today. I wish I did not. It haunts me. I will not pass those monstrous images to you. Believe me, you do not want to know. While Smith tortured the bullfrog, he talked to it almost lovingly, and chuckled to himself. Now I knew where the bodies of the bull frogs scattered around the pond had come from.

Resisting the urge to vomit, I stepped forward in front of Smith. He was surprised to see me, but smiled at me as if he had invited me to a special event.

"DeeDee! How nice of you to come. Come join the fun. I'll show you how to do it." I had already seen how he did it, and it made me ill. He rose from the squatted position he was in to stand, fat legs spread for balance.

I reached into my pocket, and snugged a roll of quarters into my fist before removing it from my pocket. When my fist exploded towards his flabby gut, the coins helped to stop my knuckles from giving, and increased the force of the blow dramatically. As he began to double up from the blow, the smile disappeared from his lips and saliva spewed from his mouth, along with all the breath in his lungs. As my boot connected with his nuts with maximum thrust, it accelerated his motion as he doubled forward. My forehead came forward and connected with his nose. I was off balance from throwing the kick, so it was not enough to do much damage..... but it was the coup de grace. He was totally incapacitated. You ever want to really hurt a guy, that's the way to do it. If you do it right, the roll of quarters might split, and it can cost you ten bucks if you don't take the time to pick them up..... but it certainly gets the job done!

I picked him up, and tossed him head first into the water. His head hit a rock as he landed on the pond's shore, and he hardly managed to struggle at all as he drowned in the shallow water.

Even though it was dead, I gently picked up the bullfrog he had tortured. I showed it the consideration it had deserved in life, and never received. I placed it in the net , being careful not to leave finger prints, and tossed it down beside Smith as if he had lost it in the fall. That's what it looked like to me: Smith had fallen while doing 'his thing' . I wanted the people who found him to know just what an ass hole he was, but doubted they would be able to figure it out. Takes an evil mind to think like him. I picked up my quarters, and the rest of the coins from my secret stash and walked away. I was never coming back. I like to think I saw a flicker of approval in those huge reptilian eyes.

The boy I had been also died there. I became a man. You might disagree, but I think a pretty good one. So. Smith's life was not a total waste, although I think the world would have been a far better place if he had never been born. I would have grown up anyway,only not quite so fast.

They found his body Monday evening, after it had been roasting in the sun for a couple of days. As I expected, it was considered an accident. Like to think he rotted enough before he was found to attract flies and feed the frogs he left behind.

We were all sent home because of the 'tragedy' My parents got a refund, which I thought was great. But, before I go on with what happened after my return from camp, I better explain myself some.

I can imagine a number of you tut tutting, thinking what kind of an evil kid kills someone at age 14?

How did he learn to fight like that? Why didn't his parents get him counselling? Send him to reform school? I'll tell you, when you are dirt poor, counselling is not an option. Reform school definitely is. But, I have never mentioned any of this before now. My parents never knew. My mother did worry that the experience of having our camp supervisor die in a tragic accident would bother me, and asked if I needed any help. She gave me a funny look when I said the guy was no loss to the world,but that is how I felt. I'm sure if we had been wealthier, I would have been sent for 'help' to adjust. I didn't need it. I did wonder if Smith had any family that grieved over him. I know I never did. Some people are worse than just a waste of space. They are like black holes in our earthly atmosphere, sucking in goodness. Smith was like that. You can judge me if you like. Will not bother me. But perhaps you should take a second to look at my point of view. Every time I see a truck go by in the middle of winter crammed full of terrified pigs on the way to slaughter, I think that although they are literally freezing both in terror and from the cold, that is probably the best day in their pathetic lives. Before that, despite the fact that they are an animal with far greater intelligence than a dog, they are kept in a pen so small they cannot lay down to rest without risking a broken leg. The vast majority of them have gone insane before this final trip. They are the lucky ones. You don't want to keep your mind sane with the life they live. Every time I see chickens on special at an obscenely cheap price, I think of the 'life' they lived to allow that price, crammed two to a cage the size of a sheet of writing paper. I could go on and on. My point: Almost everyone knows these conditions exist Huge corporations have driven out the small farmers in the never ending race to produce cheaper, faster. We know it, yet somehow our brains let us ignore the horror of it. Is killing some ass hole like Smith really that bad in comparison? Most people seem to think so. I don't.

I'd like to live a peaceful life. Really would. That's why I live in the middle of no where. If I wanted trouble I'd live in a city. Cities attract trouble makers the way shit attracts flies. Tough guys prey on the weak. Tougher guys pray on the tough guys that get rich from the weak. You probably have heard the saying "Big fleas have lesser fleas and so on ad infinitum" It was coined by a Victorian mathematician who you probably never heard of, Augustus De Morgan. . Augustus borrowed the idea from the seventeenth Century writer, Jonathan Swift. It was true in the seventeenth century, true in Victorian times, is true now. Especially in cities. Bigger the city, bigger the pyramid that the situation produces.

I try to avoid trouble. That's why I live far away from cities. But, somehow trouble keeps finding me anyway. Seems my life is destined to be long stretches of calm, enjoying happiness, enjoying life, interspersed with brief spats of violence and turmoil. Seems it is destined to always be like that. The incredible beauty of nature seems always to be at war with the incredible greed of that 1% of humanity that controls so much wealth. The 1% ers in the top echelon of our society that run the world...at least the world as seen through human eyes. The economy above all else. We are the foot soldiers, obeying their orders without question. Consuming.

Nature always seems to be losing the battles lately..... I can guarantee if it continues, she will win the war. There can be no economy without an ecology. But, I am not telling you here about my fights with those 1% ers in the top echelons, although there have been enough of them I have fought in my life. Save that for another time. Here I am going to tell you about that period in my life when I kept banging heads with a group of 1% ers from the bottom echelon, an outlaw motorcycle gang known as 'The Evil Ones'.

CHAPTER 3

The Man in Black, Johnny Cash, wrote a great song 'A boy named Sue' about a boy so named by his father so that he would grow up tough and survive the cruel world he would have to face. Being stuck with a surname like Death, growing up in a tough neighbourhood, is a bit like being named Sue. And, initials that sound like a girls name if you say them wrong, DeeDee, compounds the problem. I preferred to be called by my nick name Double D or just plain Dave. But, I had to fight to enforce that preference. As it says in the song, get tough or die.

Most people born with the surname Death like to say that their name refers to the Belgian city of Ath, and the "De" in front simply means 'of' or 'from' in French. So, using that explanation, my name would be David from Ath. Ergo, the pronunciation would be De Ath, Two syllables, with the 'e' emphasized . Sounds great, but is probably not the truth. Our ancestors are not from Belgium or France. The ancestors of people with the name Death aren't. The name actually comes from ancestors who played the part of 'Death' in popular English medieval plays. My dad is a stickler for the truth. So, my family pronounces it 'Death' and be damned. Kids pounce on a chance like that to ridicule another kid.

My old man must have gone through it. He's a great

guy that fought professionally as a boxer for a few years. Heavyweight. Killer Ken. Must have got into fighting as a pro 'cause he was good at it as a kid. He could have really made it big I reckon, but a car accident took his left leg from the knee down at an early age, ending his career and making gainful employment almost impossible...although he sure did try. Most of the time he got work as a security guard at minimum wage, and tinkered in his spare time, doing renovations, repairing things for people. He was good at it, but did not have the equipment to do it in a big way. Lots of guys faced with what he had to face would have turned to booze and taken it out on the wife and kid. Not dad. He just sort of turned inward. No man could have broken his spirit, but I think the loss of a leg made him feel he was not a real man anymore. I have always thought he was way more man than most. So does my mum, Cathy. She helped him when she could with renovations, and was pretty handy in her own right, but working as a waitress at a local restaurant and looking after the house left her pretty tired. Thirty years married now, they still love each other. My mum is an incredible woman...but I guess most guys feel like that. I reckon, in my case it is true. Incredible hardships, incredible disappointments..... never a complaint. She always kept her sense of humour. God knows how. I love her for it. I love my wife, but my mum will always be the other woman in my life.

I was a handful for my parents up to my fourteen birthday. They knew I loved and respected them, but

I had a mind of my own. Smart, iron strong, iron willed, fast as a hungry dog stealing food off an unattended table, and pugnacious. I was fortunate in that I was always very big for my age, far bigger than my dad was at comparable ages. That was an asset, as I got into a lot of fights. Took me a little while to realize that fighting fair was important in the ring, but fighting to win was important in the day to day world. When fights were one on one, I won 'em all. Won most of 'em when it was two against one also. Fighting fair is fine if both sides agree to the concept. In street fights they rarely do. The guys I grew up with had a motto: "Put in the nut, kick in the nuts." The latter is self evident. The biggest, toughest guy is down for the count if he is the recipient of a kick to the cajoles. The former refers to using your head as a battering ram, your bent legs as a driving force to spring forwards. The forehead's shape and lack on anything over it but skin makes it tough. If you doubt me, try breaking an egg between thumb and middle finger, the egg end to end. Impossible. The forehead is like that. It is like that to protect the brain. If you want to protect your ass, learn to use your brain's protector when you are in a down and dirty fight. Far better than a fist any day. One forehead butt, and the fight is over. As a kid, you will probably break the other kids nose. As an adult, you have a good chance of killing the guy, driving shards of broken bone into his brain. Better be careful if that bothers you.

In public school kids quickly learned it was not smart to mess with me. Then I graduated to high school, and had to start educating the other kids, all over again. Testosterone is starting to rage through the teenage body in the high school years, and you are mixed in with kids all the way up to seventeen or eighteen. I entered grade nine at thirteen. I took on a couple of seniors and was left alone pretty much after that.

Learning had never been a problem. Kept my parents happy with A's in public school without ever having to study. Saw no reason to change in high school, so sat in the back rows of all my classes , in with the struggling sixteen year olds, who were just waiting to finish school so they could get a fill job in until they turned eighteen and headed down the mines. Some of them were bullies. Soon sorted them out. The other guys were OK. I arm wrestled for quarters when no teacher was looking, and made lunch money. After school they taught me poker and pool. In poker, I found something that really interested me, something I was born for. I studied poker, reading every book I could get on strategies, and learning to read every gesture, every facial tick.

Pretty soon I was making almost as much as my dad did in his job! But, I was playing against older kids who did not appreciate a young kid cleaning them out. I got into more than my share of fights. Managed to win em all except when on those rare occasions when three or four kids would jump me.

I was really starting to worry my parents, as I stayed out late and always seemed to be recovering from scrapes and bruises. That summer, as I turned fourteen, they sent me off to a summer camp for two weeks, even though I know they could not afford it. I should have helped them out financially at that point, but I was just a kid. In much less than two weeks, I came back as a man. But, you already know about that.

I live by my own code. Have since I was fourteen. I did a hell of a lot of thinking that year, trying to make sense of the world. Sorted a lot of things out. You may not agree with some things I do, but I assure they are not done without thought. I am true to my code. I sleep well most nights.

People that know me know that they can say what they like to me. I take that old 'sticks and stones may break my bones' saying to heart. Words will never hurt me. The wrong actions on your part can get you into a world of hurt with me real fast....but words? Far as I am concerned, you can have an opinion on anything, no matter how stupid, or call me anything, no matter how insulting. You might as well give me your opinion. You are going to get mine. That's how we learn. I wasn't always like that. Up to the age of fourteen I had a chip on my shoulder and dared people to knock it off. Now, I encourage people to speak their mind, and practice the same freedom myself. That way, you know where you stand. I take freedom of speech to heart.

Usually I avoid subjects like politics and religion with people I do not know or people I know have opinions diametrically opposed to mine. They aint gonna hurt my feelings, but it saves a lot of hurt feelings on their part. But, since I am telling you so much about myself here, there will be times I tread on a few toes. As Polonius said in Hamlet, "This above all else, to thine own self be true." I know most of you will disagree with what I say, indeed with what I do. I ask however that you do not judge me without waiting until you see why I feel the way that I do. I will explain as I go along. I don't expect you to change your minds, but try to keep an open one. I promise you I am always true to myself.

When it comes to religion, Frank Lloyd Wright expressed it best for me: "I believe in God, only I spell it nature." Before I went to that camp, I had always gone to church with my parents. Even before my coming of age, I had trouble digesting what the church was trying to feed me. I had no problem with the commandment to honour my father and mother Good people. Good commandment. But some of the others? They just did not jibe with with what I saw. People talked about them, didn't follow them. Could never understand the hypocrisy. Never could accept something just because I was told it was so, so I studied the Bible some. A lot of people spout off without even reading it. I read it. Just don't agree with most of it. Out of the Ten Commandments, I only find 3 of them worthwhile.

(See notes on David's religious beliefs on page 224)

CHAPTER 4

Months of introspection when I got home, drastically changed my life and my attitudes. One of the first things I did was lie to my parents. It was something I rarely did, but I knew they would never accept that I made a living gambling, so I told them I had landed a job at the pool hall. If you wanted to rationalize it, that was technically correct: the room where the local gamblers played poker was in the back of the pool hall. Told them I wanted to help with the household expenses, seeing as how, as a growing boy, I was eating them out of house and home.

Another thing I did, was lose the chip on my shoulder and learned to lose . Sometimes I would deliberately lose at poker. Other times I would win at poker only to lose half of it back at pool. I did not have to try to lose at pool...It came naturally to me. Not my game. I just made certain that at the end of the week I was ahead. Basically, I stopped fighting. I did a lot of thinking about how incredibly easy it was for me to kill Smith. Both the actual task and the lack of remorse. Figured I had to be REALLY careful to control that.... would be too easy to get out of hand and kill for the wrong reasons. Thought then, and think now, removing him from the planet was a good thing. But. This was a thing that required a very tight rein indeed. I stopped fighting unless it was absolutely necessary, and made certain to hold back some when it was.

Joined a gym. I had so much testosterone roaring through my body, found I was getting together with Mrs Palmer and her five daughters three or four times every night, and was still waking up in the morning from wet dreams. Prefer to sleep in the raw, but back then had no choice but to wear pyjama bottoms. Cleaning up that mess was my first chore every morning..... not the sort of thing you want your mum to have to do...... I figured pumping weights would help me to not pump my python. Not so sure it helped in that regard, but found that I loved working out. Arnold Schwarzenegger, in the movie "Pumping Iron" said the feeling he got from working out was like the feeling of coming in sex . He either had incredibly lousy sex, or those incredible drugs he took enhanced the feelings he had working out. I'll never know. To me the two feelings are not even close. But I do enjoy the feeling working out gives me. I never took enhancement drugs. Never needed them. At 6'1", I'm 230 lbs these days. At sixteen I was 190 lbs and one of the strongest in the gym.

To the delight of my parents, I took an interest in a couple of school subjects....English Composition and English Literature. I still manged 70's in the other subjects without studying, but shot to the top in those two classes. I started writing short stories about nature. Even managed to get a few published. But, a man could starve trying to live off such stories.

They were not so delighted with my other new-found love: motorcycles! Most of the guys I had shared the back seats with in grade nine were now out in the world. Most of them were going nowhere , and they knew it. Most of them knew society had no time for them, so they delighted in giving society the finger. They knew they were on the road to nowhere, and figured they might as well travel in style. Motorcycles seem to fit that style nicely. They drifted into bike gangs.... the type that attracted the guys who loved to ride and party. Yes, they got into trouble, but nothing serious.

I had absolutely no intention of following the same road they did. But, I found I loved the thrill of a big bike. Even though I was only fourteen I was big for my age, and they let me ride their bikes and taught me how to do it properly. By the time I was sixteen I was better than most of them at riding. Good balance, steady nerves and fast reflexes helped a lot. All the guys had riding names. Johnny suggested Paladin as a name for me. He was called Bullwhip when he was riding with the other guys. God knows where he got that name ..... I told him Bull**shit** would be more like it. He just smiled.
"Go fuck yourself Double D. The name Paladin suits you. My old man has a bunch of DVD's of a series he used to watch on the box, back when he was a kid called 'Have Gun, Will Travel.' This guy, a gunslinger back in the days of the wild west, travels from place to place hiring himself out to kill people.

He makes the rich ass holes pay big time for his help, but helps out regular folk for free. A tough son of a bitch with a heart of gold. That's you Double D. You'd help anybody out...and you sure kill those rich guys when you play poker! That's you, a killer with a heart. Paladin"

I had never told Johnny about the incident at Whispering Pines. You don't talk about such things. Johnny was not a friend, but even if he had been, I would not have mentioned it. Friends can become enemies. I smiled inwardly at the irony of being called a killer with a heart, and agreed to come over to his place and watch this show.

Paladin was a cool guy. Richard Boone who starred as Paladin, and directed the whole thing had no muscle to speak of..... but when you have a big gun and know how to use it, I guess you really don't need muscle. I didn't like his looks, but I liked his attitude. I borrowed the whole series, and watched them all. I looked up the name Paladin and found that Paladins were warriors of Charlemagne's court who were renowned for heroism and chivalry. Have to admit that appealed to my ego. From then on, my nickname was Paladin.

I made it to seventeen and the end of high school without incident. Time to leave the nest. I had good marks and my parents wanted me to go to University. But, that definitely wasn't for me, and I think they knew that. They took it well when I told them I was heading to the big city for a while. Not that I like big cities ..... but I had to find out what the world was all about. As Liza said :"If You Can Make it There, You Can Make it Anywhere" Yep. That song was written for and first performed by Liza Minnelli. Most people think Frank Sinatra..... but Frank was 'connected', so stealing the glory was no biggie I guess. Of course it was also about New York City and I sure wasn't going there! Some people love cities. I can't see the appeal.

Hardrock, the town I grew up in, was about 25,000 people. Even that was far too big for my taste. For a large portion of the population it seems that making money is the be all and end all of existence. Money has never been that important to me, but a man has to live. Unless I wanted to move down the mines, I knew I'd never make enough to live the way I wanted to live if I stayed in Hardrock. People will only lose so much to a guy playing poker in a small town. Had to get out and try my luck elsewhere. But, the city I had in mind was about 500,000 people . That was about 490,000 more than I was comfortable with, but had to be done. Hardrock is a mining town. The city I moved to was nick named Steeltown. for the big smelters. Same sort of place, only bigger.

I stayed in Steeltown for a few years. I did not make it there.. but I survived. In Steeltown I first met the group known as the Evil Ones. Survival took on a whole new meaning. I soon realized I had to make it out of there to make a new life elsewhere or I would not survive at all. I had better explain.

CHAPTER 5

First thing I did when I arrived in the city was buy a bike. Harley Davidsons are very nice, and to my eyes can be works of art when they are customized..... but they cost a fortune to buy, a fortune to customize, and a fortune to insure if you are only 17. I had a nice little nest egg from my days 'working' at the pool hall, but not enough for that. I had a lot of friends in my home town that would have had given me a chopped Harley for a really good price, but the bike would for certain have had a dubious lineage, and I would have left my parents worried sick if I had left home on something like that. I figured what they did not know would not worry them. Well, not as much. I bought an older Yamaha 750 Virago. Johnny had provided me with the names of guys in Steeltown I could trust to do a good job of customizing. I had them extend the front end 5 inches, increase the rake, drop the rear end down , add a fat tire on the back, and remove all mention of Yamaha. I had the tank painted black to match the frame, and had them put the name 'Hardly Davidson's' in gold prominently on both sides of the tank, using the Harley script. Harley Davidson could sue me if they liked. I had a bike I was proud of for a fraction of the cost. Harley Davidson had made millions cashing in on the bad boy image. I doubted very much they would care what a seventeen year old did to cash in on their image .

Next thing was a gym. By then I was addicted to the feeling I got working out. And, I needed a gym to make connections. I found myself what is known as a muscle head gym .... cheap, no fancy machines. Just the basics, and tons of free weight. Just the sort of place to work out seriously, and to meet the kind of guys I needed. I found a small furnished two room apartment nearby, and I was all set. I could have got just a room a lot cheaper, but I needed a kitchen. I like to cook. Much prefer to cook myself than eat the fast food junk most people eat. For years I had made my own bread, and helped my mom make shepherd's pie and casseroles. Super soups too. She was a gifted cook and gave me great recipes. I wanted to start making my own wine and beer too. So, I needed a kitchen. Damned if I was going to start eating like the sickly people I saw around me in the city, too busy chasing money to find the time to cook for themselves. Wasn't going to eat like a bodybuilder either. I loved working out, but I liked good healthy food, desserts and alcohol. I figured I could eat and drink what I liked and as much as I liked, as long as I worked out hard enough. I enjoyed having a good body, but no way I was ever going to be prancing around on a stage in a skimpy bathing suit showing off my cuts and my muscles. Cant think of many things I would want to do less. So, watching my intake was not in the cards.

I had some money, but I needed a way to make more. What I had would not last forever. Making money at poker games would have to wait until I had made the correct connections. I had looked into this before I made the move. Looked at Internet poker and looked at what is called curb-siding. Internet poker is a joke. Talking of jokes, it reminds me of one I heard years ago :

A cowboy rides into a new town and asks the first person he sees where he can find a poker game. The guy says " Everyone in this town plays poker at Joe's Bar. It's the only game in town. I have to tell you, though; you'll lose everything. Everyone knows the game is fixed. "
"If everyone know it's fixed, why does everyone play there?" he replied.
"I told you! It's the only game in town."

Do you really think games online can't be fixed? REALLY?

I'm not bragging, but I know poker. All the odds, all the moves, all the games. I actually prefer games like Stud and Omaha, but these days no limit Holdem is all the rage. So, we'll talk that. Sure , you can win the nickel and dime games sometimes online , and if you are good, you can play 12 hours a day and make 30 or 40 bucks on average. You have to average it out. Poker is like that...some days you win, some days you lose..... it is the long haul that matters. But, chances are, you don't want to spend week after week playing twelve hours a day so that you can make less than minimum wage. So, you will probably start playing bigger games with bigger payouts. Get into the tournaments with those nice payouts beckoning you to try your luck. Funny thing happens. Sure as shit you will get ahead if you know how to play. Then you are going to get AA or AK suited. Your gonna raise, and some other position at the table is gonna call all in. What are you going to do? Fold one of the best hands you can start with? As Kenny Rogers points out in 'The Gambler' "Every hands a winner, and every hands a loser". So, what do you do?

Many is the time in a real game I have started with AA , raised, and then folded after those first 3 cards, the flop, hit the table. Especially if I have just sat down, I'll do it if I don't like what I see on the flop. Couple of kings flop, and a guy goes all in, I'm leery. He might have three kings. Could even have a full house. Still might call him, but I am definitely gonna think about it. I just sat down and started to play. Do I want to lose everything I brought to the table that soon?

After I have been playing a guy for a while, hell, I may fold if three low cards of the same suit appear on the flop. That is what winning at poker is all about. The mechanics of the game are second nature to me. What I am doing while I play is studying my opponents. I'll joke around if the guys want to, act like I don't care if necessary, even act drunk. Don't you believe it. The Jesuits say " Give me the child until he is seven and I care not who has him thereafter" I say " give me a poker player for fifteen minutes, and 99% of the time I can tell you what his hand is like". His fate is sealed, just like the fate of that poor schmuck the Jesuits control. If I think he has a couple of cards of the same suit that flopped, unless I have the ace of that suit in my hand, I'm folding. Even if I have the ace of that suit, I may fold. Depends on how much that all in is going to hurt me. I still have to have another card of that suit turn up to make the highest flush, and there are only two more coming. If it's going to cost me my stack, I'm probably folding. Takes thousands of games under your belt to make those kind of decisions wisely.

Getting back to that online game. You raised to let everyone know you had a good hand, and this other position went all in. You will note I say position. We are online here.... I am not convinced all those 'seats' are taken by an individual. Yep, you can 'talk' to each other in online games.... but you cant see each other. Call me suspicious, but I can see a guy sitting at a desk, controlling things, playing the part of ten different guys on ten different tables. You call his all in and he shows ten jack off suit. A weak hand. Why the hell would he call all in with that? Then the flop comes. Nine, queen king. One of the other 2 cards may be an ace.... but you have three of a kind, and "he" has a straight. You lose. Yes, it can happen in a live game...that's poker. But not nearly as often as it does online. What kind of an idiot goes all in with ten jack off suit? I reckon usually an idiot that knows the outcome already. You'd have a hard time convincing me the games online are not fixed.

You like the thrill of playing with "the big guys" online? Good luck to you! Personally, I think you would have far better luck going to a casino and playing roulette. In America, with the double zero wheel, the odds are 5.26% against you. Lets face it. Most casinos are run by the mob, directly or indirectly. But, they are run fairly in most of the big casinos. They know that with 5.26% running against you with every spin of the wheel, you play long enough, and unless you are incredibly lucky, and smart enough to quit when you are ahead, they are gonna win. Win everything you have. In my opinion, you have better odds on casino roulette, than you do on online poker. As I said , just my opinion.

So, I could not make a living playing on line. Knew that . I decided to start curb-siding. That is street talk for buying and selling cars from your home .... In my case it would not be cars, I had done my research and conversion camper vans were the thing to deal in.

Steeltown is about 40 miles from the Queenston/Lewiston bridge into the USA. At the time I moved there our Canadian dollar was worth more than the USA greenback. That does not happen too often, It opens opportunities for importing when it does. I had researched on line and found that there were incredible deals to be had on conversion vans in the US, vehicles being sold on eBay. I had already searched out reliable companies to buy from and had made myself familiar with the paperwork and procedures required. Simple enough. Had to bid on a succession of conversion vans to get the deal I wanted, but within a week I was the proud owner of a 5 year old Savana Conversion van with only 30,000 miles on it. Really nice van! Bought it on line, made sure the seller notified the US border that I was bringing it across, and provided a copy of the ownership to them, as required by US law. That first deal went so easy I was lulled into a false sense of security. Made an easy $4,000 profit, and made the guy that bought it very happy to get a deal. Win, win all around.

When I got back with that first vehicle, I found a familiar chopped Harley sitting outside my apartment. Johnny was hanging around waiting for my return. He had decided that he was not going to get anywhere in Hardrock either, and had come to see how I was making out. Could not have come at a better time for him. I was high on my first success, and explained it to him. I knew that any more than 6 vehicles a year and the government would start getting suspicious....curb siding is a no no without a dealer's license. There is an old expression. "DO NOT STEAL! The Government does not like the competition!" The government makes money by selling dealer licences.... and it's best not to mess with the government, unless you have to. There were plenty of vans to go around. Told Johnny we could alternate. I'd find the vans to buy ...I was good at finding the deals, and had the necessary funds. I would sell them. I got on OK with Johnny....but he was a poster boy for that old expression: 'Would you buy a used car from this man?' Most people would not. In return, Johnny would do any necessary repairs to the vehicles, something he was good at. He was as happy as the proverbial pig in shit. I told him he could stay at my place for the night, but I prized my privacy. Next day he got his own. He understood.

Later, I asked him to help me find some poker games I could play in. He said he would keep it in mind. I knew Johnny. Lots of friends in low places, and if he didn't know now, he soon would. I had floated him the bucks to buy his first van, but he had soon made enough to pay me back. He had found a connection to buy weed in bulk and with the profit from his first van he was in business dealing dope. He was learning the ins and outs of dealing in steroids too. That was Johnny. I don't judge.

Things went great for the first seven vehicles. Four for me, three for Johnny. Every time we came back with one we would ride our bikes out to a little place we had found outside Steeltown, Frank's diner. Frank was a taciturn man, with what seemed like the same dirty apron always around his fat waist. But, he sure could cook. The food was fantastic. Hardly anyone was ever in the place for breakfast when we went. Gather the place was busy at lunch and supper, when Frank had a waitress on duty to serve the customers and he stayed in the kitchen. The man could cook, but his appearance would not instill confidence in customers, and I think he knew that. For breakfast though, it was just him, All the times we went there, he never made any attempt to get to know us. Only spoke to us to find out what we were ordering. I always figured he was the kind of guy that minded his own business and expected others to do the same. That suited us just fine. Later, I figured out when he saw us ride up on bikes, he figured we were members of The Evil Ones, whose club house was nearby, and that was why he kept his distance.

Frank's was on the main road out of Steeltown at an intersection with a small country road that was one S curve after another as it wound it's way alongside a river, and through a swamp. 20 miles of winding road and gentle hills. Great views, and a perfect place for a bike ride. Many's the time we went roaring around those curves, foot pegs touching the asphalt and sending up showers of sparks as we leaned into the curves. When you are young,you think you are invincible. It is a wonder one of us did not kill ourselves ; the road was not really in the best of shape and one wrong connection with a bump at the speeds we were doing, would have sent us for a messy ride through the swamp. I almost always won the races. Not because I was better than Johnny. He was a damned good bike rider. But a Yamaha handles better than a Harley. Motorcycle gangs all drive Harleys because of the image..... there are much better handling, more dependable, faster bikes out there, for less money.

Everything was going great. I had bought number eight in Johnny's name. Bought it from a Cleveland dealer I had dealt with before. Good to deal with. I got him to fax a copy of the ownership to US border as required, and had him send a copy to me. A cautious type, I liked to fax one off myself as a safety precaution, to avoid problems. We set off to Cleveland to pick the van up. We did not drive there....bikes like ours attract the wrong attention. Besides, we would have had to put one of them in the van....bad idea with a clean conversion van. We always took the Greyhound, and drove the van back.

I didn't expect any problems. I have since learned that problems usually come when you don't expect them.

(For some of David's recipes, see Page 227)

CHAPTER 6

I got a call from my dad in the evening, after we had picked up the van. Mum was having trouble with her stomach and had to go in for tests. Dad does not have a car. He say's it is because of his leg, but I reckon he just can't afford one. The tests were in a city, close to a hundred miles away. No direct bus service, it would take them most of the day to get there. I told him I was in the States, but not to worry. I would be home around 2 pm tomorrow. Dad knows I would not let him down. He sounded a lot less stressed when I hung up.

Usually, we partied after picking up a van..... great party vehicles. You meet a girl and want to take her back to your place....your place is just outside in the parking lot. I explained my problem to Johnny and we decided to drive through the night, and sleep in the van just outside Buffalo. That way we could be one of the first across the border once the office for vehicle clearance opened. Should be no problem...home by eleven. Or, so I thought.

We arrived at the Queenston/Lewiston bridge shortly after their 8am opening, hoping to clear Johnny's vehicle quickly, There was one person ahead of me. From the extremely rude way he was being treated I assumed he must have done something very wrong.

I knew *I* was in for a difficult time when the woman turned to me, scowled at me, and snapped "where is your vehicle?" casting her eyes back to papers on her desk. It was Johnny's vehicle, but I usually do the talking. Johnny can get himself into trouble pretty quick by mouthing off. I assumed that she was still angry from whatever the man in front of me had done, and politely answered "it is that one there" as I pointed to it. You could see it from the window. Best to tread gently. The question was asked again, louder, sharper, still without looking up. I replied the same way. There were no numbers on the parking spaces that I could see...I knew of no other way to tell her. There weren't that many vehicles out there Third time, louder still, still looking down, hands braced on the table as if she was having trouble controlling her anger. I replied the same way, adding that I was pointing to it... you can see it from the window. I could hear Johnny getting agitated, and turned to him, mouthed the words "keep out of it." She still did not look out the window, but approached the desk and snatched the ownership from me. She flipped though some papers on the desk and announced: "You did not fax a copy of the ownership." I informed her that a copy had been faxed. Indeed, it had been faxed twice. Once by me, once by the dealer we bought from. "You don't need to fax it twice you shit. You like wasting our time? When was it faxed the first time?" Unsure, I said Monday or Tuesday of the previous week. "You have to give me the exact time!" I am starting to get rattled at this point. I had no idea why she was acting this way. I was anxious to get home, did not want any trouble, and really could not think exactly which day. I guessed Monday. I guessed wrong. She produced a list of faxes received. Looked at it, then showed me. "No record of it here. You cannot export the vehicle. Come back in three days" I asked her to check Tuesday. I was told that she did not have time for this. I would have to re-submit the paperwork and return in 3 days. I explained I had to be home due to a medical emergency. She laughed. "You shits. You are all the same. 'I have a sick mother'. 'I have a sick baby'. 'I have a medical emergency'.....your excuses are weak. Really weak." Desperate, I asked her to please check Tuesday. Making it obvious that it was a great effort she got another file, flipped though quickly not really looking, and not showing it to me. "No, not there" She tossed the file back on her desk. For the first time she smiled.... it was not a pleasant smile.

"You cannot export the vehicle. Re-submit, and come back in 3 days." The look said it all. She was enjoying herself. No use arguing. She had the power and she was enjoying it to the max.

"What am I supposed to do?"

"I already told you. Re-submit. Come back in three days. I am finished with you."

"Where am I supposed to go?"
"I don't care where you go, you shit. Just leave."

The man she had been abusing before I came in saw I was confused, and whispered a suggestion. Her venomous look as he tried to help silenced him, but he had said enough to give me a rough idea..... I left him to her venom, feeling sorry for him, but powerless to do anything. As I walked out the door I heard her laying into him.

"Listen you little shit. When I tell you to talk, you talk. Otherwise you keep your shitty mouth shut. Got that? You fucking rag heads are all the same."

I found the place the man had whispered the name of to me about a mile down the road. Marshall Towing. . When I explained the bizarre encounter, the owner of the compound said "Ah. You had to deal with 'The Blonde'. She is famous here. Nasty, nasty piece of work. To her everyone is a shit. Her favourite expression. Think it makes her feel important to call everybody that. The guy who's balls she was busting was poor old Mohammed. Works for me taking vehicles across and back. Guess I can expect him back here soon.... she wont let him across today. I'll send another driver with the vehicle tomorrow afternoon. She often uses that 'the fax was never received' on you Canadians. Knows it leaves you in a real bind. Like I said, that woman is as mean as they come."

I was told it would cost $10 a day to keep the truck there. The man was kind enough to make another copy of the ownership that I could hand in when I went back to the border, and even arranged a ride for us with a driver that was going there. It turned out this driver had suffered through many encounters with 'The Blonde' . He said he had several times complained to her supervisor, and suggested I see him. I was told the supervisors name was Bob, and he was a fair man....but the driver doubted he was truly aware of the treatment being dished out in the vehicle export office.

"That bitch can be all smiles and sweetness when she wants to be. Doubt Bob ever sees the person we have to deal with. Bet she's totally different with him. I thought at first she just hated men, but it is not that. I see her just about every Friday evening down at The Sunset Bar. Knocks back the G and T's pretty good for a woman her size. All smiles and chuckles, and she usually leaves half sloshed with a guy. Usually one of about three or four she likes to play against each other. She's not bad looking really, but I would not fuck her with **your** dick! Nastiest piece of work I've ever seen. Power of the job really brings out the worst in her. All smiles and chuckles away from the job though. Pity the poor bastard that marries that."

I saw the supervisor, complained about the treatment, and dropped off my copy of the ownership with him, expressing my fear that it too might disappear if I had to take it back into the export office. He promised to have a word with the lady concerned , and said he would drop the ownership copy off personally. Nice enough guy. Throughout it all, Johnny remained silent. I had asked him to, as I had to get back for my mum's sake. I could tell he was fuming inside, but not a word passed his lips.

We waited for the driver to finish his paperwork so that he could drive us across to the Canadian side, as he had said he would. He'd said he would have no problems...she only pulled her stunts on one driver from their business at a time to avoid making it obvious. He was right. While waiting I mulled over my situation. It suddenly dawned on me that our temporary permit may expire before I could return! I expressed this fear to the driver as we crossed the bridge, and he suggested I go in and talk to the Canadian customs people while he saw his broker. I did. I explained the situation and was amazed to find out that they also knew of 'The Blonde'! They were most understanding ,sympathetic and helpful. They explained that we could not walk back over the bridge to the vehicle to check...we would be arrested if we walked on the bridge. US customs no longer allowed foot traffic. They told me that they could not help me with getting back across the bridge, but if I could get back and decided to bring the vehicle over now, without US clearance, they would issue me my Form 1,the required Canadian form for import .

"That faxing a copy of the ownership to the border is a US regulation. We don't care. You get the vehicle here, we'll clear you. We have done it numerous times for people that ran into her. Can't say what problems it will get you into with the US if you try to bring another vehicle in later, but we'll get this one in for you, no problem."

I told Johnny to stay put, talk to no one, stay out of trouble. He nodded, not saying a word. I could tell he was fuming, but he knew better than to go against my wishes. I can understand people's reluctance to give a ride to an unknown person who wants to cross a border. So, numerous attempts to hitch a ride failed miserably. Then I managed to arrange transport over to the USA side with a sympathetic Canadian border worker, who had heard my story, and who also knew of "The Blonde" This lady was indeed well known. Told me he spent his day driving back and forth with papers. Driving me across would present no problem.... but I would have to check in with the US side immediately when I got there. He did not want any trouble. Fair enough.

I spoke to the same supervisor, Bob, and said I wanted to go back to my vehicle to get some things. He explained that even though the vehicle impound I needed to reach was within walking distance, I would have to take a taxi to the vehicle. He was apologetic, but that was the law. No one was allowed to walk away from the border. Never did figure out the reason for that. Did they think terrorists were more likely to attack on foot? I was in no position to argue. The taxi company saw me coming. They must have loved 'the Blonde'. Good for business. Charged me $50. They knew they had me by the short and curlies. Hmm. Maybe 'the

Blondes' father was a taxi driver.....

When I reached the vehicle, I determined that the temporary license would indeed now expire before I could clear the vehicle. I discussed it with the owner, explained my urgency. He suggested I just try to drive across to the Canadian side. Said they had cameras but would not be looking for me. Made sense. I did so without incident. No charge for the short stay in his compound. I thanked him, and just drove right on past the building where 'The Blonde' was, the building where I was supposed to check in. Just drove past as part of the crowd of traffic at that time of day.

True to their word, the Canadian side had me on our way faster than usual. All the way home Johnny never said a word. When I dropped him off, he could hold it no longer.

"Fuck Paladin, that was just not right! I know you have to get back for your mum's sake, but that bitch should have been put in her place. Fucking cow. No one should treat you or me that way. Not right!" By then, Johnny was the only one that called me Paladin. To me it sounded kind of pompous.... so to everyone else I was Dave or Double D.

"You just cool off Johnny. Don't you worry. I am not going to just let it slide. When I get back I'll explain. I have plans for our blonde friend. She's going to regret calling everyone a shit. We'll teach her the meaning of the word. Go to the gym, work off the anger. I need to borrow your new van. I'll be back tomorrow."

Johnny nodded, a puzzled look starting to replace the anger. Johnny knew I never made idle threats. I looked at him and smiled.

"Hey Johnny. How do you keep an idiot in suspense?" When he did not respond, still looking puzzled, I replied " I'll tell you tomorrow."

He got the joke, and it left him with a smile on his face. I took off fast to make it in time to pick up my parents.

Mum turned out fine. She'd had trouble with her stomach on and off for years. Nerves. The specialist examined her, changed her medicine, and sent her on her way. I never told them of the problems. Why bother them for nothing? Dropped them off, kissed mum goodbye, and high fived my dad. I made one stop on the way back to the city, to pick up something from an old poker buddy.

First place I went was Johnny's. "Johnny. What do you say we teach our blonde friend that payback is a bitch"

"What do you have in mind,Paladin?"

"Well, first you have to understand that you may have problems at the border from now on, once they catch on to what we did. Damned if I know what the repercussions are, but we ran their border. Luck of the draw, the van was in your name. So any trouble coming down the pipe will be on you. Sorry. Nothing I can do about that."

"I don't give a fuck about that,Paladin. Had enough of wheeling and dealing in vans anyway. Other irons in the fire. Dope business is doing good, and that steroid stuff is really taking off. Started taking it myself. You see a difference?"

"Thought you were beefing up pretty fast Johnny. I'd tell you to be careful, but know you would not listen anyway. Just as long as you understand the problems you may have later. Steroids fuck your body up long term." He just smirked. Like I said, I knew he would not listen.

"At this moment the fact we jumped the border stop without the right papers is no problem. Word of what we did wont work through the system that fast. Tomorrow is Friday. I figured you and I would go down to Buffalo and visit 'The Sunset Bar' the driver talked about. With any luck our friend will be there. I want to buy her a drink."

Johnny looked at me puzzled. "What's on your mind?"

"Well, do you remember old Bart? Not a bad poker player, but he had a real problem with the drink. He'd get pissed and lose his shirt. I stopped playing with him if he had been drinking , tried to stop him from playing when I saw he was sauced. Nice old guy. Felt sorry for him. I don't need to make money that way. Not from someone I know. Then, all of a sudden he started to come to the games sober. I asked him how he did it. Told me he had been to see his doctor. Explained he had real trouble not drinking, and his doctor gave him some pills call 'Antabuse' Doctor told him if he took one he must not drink for at least 8 hours. If he did he would get extreme diarrhoea and would be vomiting for days. No lasting health affects, but a brutal reaction.

Bart being Bart, he had to try it to be convinced. Said it was the worst two days of his life..... spewing out from both ends. Could hardly stand up. That experience worked like a charm for him. All he had to do was take a pill before the game and the very thought of a drink made him queasy. Rest of the time he could drink as he pleased. I reckon if we can introduce 'The Blonde' to this experience she may think twice before she calls someone else a shit. I dropped in and saw Bart on the way home and he gave me a couple"

Poor Johnny. Could not stop laughing for a few minutes....said he could not wait for tomorrow to come!

We borrowed a car from a friend. Once again, our bikes may have caused problems, and we damn sure could not use the van. Seven pm we headed for Buffalo.

We found 'The Sunset Bar' around nine thirty. I told Johnny to grab himself a beer, but keep it down to a minimum. I would not be drinking at all. I had to drive back across the border.

We were in luck. 'The Blonde' was already there. She was happy and smiling and hanging off the arm of some guy, winking and waving to a couple of others. She and her date had been drinking quite a bit already....you could tell by the way they moved on the dance floor. They had left two almost empty drinks on their table. I decided to buy them both a drink . G and T for the little lady, with a little extra just her. A fresh beer for the date. He looked like a bit of an ass hole, but I had nothing against him. So, it was just a regular beer. I figured I owed him that, 'cause because of me he sure wasn't going to get lucky tonight.

When they came back to the table they never even noticed they had fresh drinks. They were already too far in the bag to notice. Never thanked me. But, I did not want any thanks anyway. They knocked back the drinks within the next half hour , and this time the guy ordered a couple more. 'The Blonde' was starting to look a little pale, but they headed for the dance floor all the same.

Never seen anything like that before. Blondie spewed her guts out all over the guy. Then she put her hands on her backside. I could only imagine what was going on there. The guy got away from her as fast as he could, leaving her to her own devices. Told you he looked like an ass hole. She staggered outside, an unbelievable mess all over her front . We walked out behind her. Johnny kept saying he could not wait to kick the shit out of her. I told him to leave her alone or he would have to deal with me. He was not happy about it, could see him boiling over to inflict pain.... but he knew better. He knew if he put the boots to her, he would get far worse from me.

Truth is, I felt sorry for her. I had not expected such a violent reaction. I knew that she took great pleasure in humiliating the people she dealt with every day, but it did not make me feel better about humiliating her. I did not tell Johnny that, and I sure as hell would not tell her. But, there it was.

She looked up at us with eyes full of horror at what was happening to her. Don't think she actually saw us. She was far, far too busy with her present problems to pay much attention. Then she farted. Bad idea....but I guess she could not help it. A very wet fart indeed. People were walking out of the club,giving her a wide berth. No one was helping her. Boyfriend had totally abandoned her.

I walked over. "I'll call you a cab. Know that is a lot more than you would do for anyone, but what the hell. He may not take you....you really stink bad lady. But, if he wont, he'll call you a cop or an ambulance. Enjoy. Oh. And next time you think of calling someone a little shit, think twice. Being nice to people can get you places. Being a bitch can come back to haunt you."

We walked away before she could recognize us. I knew what I had said would stick and she would know it was payback, but I did not want her to know from who exactly. There were probably hundreds of guys that wanted their own back. Let her guess. I called her a cab. I knew the effects would wear off in a day or so, but the memory would stay with her for a long long time.

Looking back, it was then that we Johnny and I started to drift far apart . I knew Johnny spent most of his time with the 1% er biker gang, The Evil Ones. The actual name of the gang was 'Evil Crew' . But, Outlaw bike gang members are called one percenters, and wear a patch that says 1% So, everyone called them the Evil Ones. Think they knew is was a better name, and revelled in it. I loved bikes, and had even thought of myself as a 1% er when I was younger. But these guys sounded like they were the real deal, real bad dudes. Besides, I was I was moving in a different direction. Johnny was going fast as he could to catch up with them.

Not so sure that the 1% ers of the biker world are the most dangerous 1% ers we should be concerned with. In fact I know they are not. But they are what I am concerned with here. I tend to go on rants sometimes..... but you've got to admit stuff like that is worth thinking about.
In the last few years, clubs such as the Bandidos, The Outlaws, the Pagan's, the Mongols, and the

Hells Angels have been gobbling up the other 1% er clubs. There is big money in drugs, prostitution and extortion. Big always wants more. No more are such big organizations just a bunch of wild guys letting off steam. They are huge money making concerns. Smaller clubs are told they will be absorbed by one of the big boys (the term is patched over) or face extinction in other ways. They patch over. These boys don't play nice. And, once you are in the big leagues, usually there is only one way out.,

Somehow the Evil Ones had not been patched over yet. Guess because they were a one chapter gang in a relatively small city. Small potatoes. I had never met the Evil ones, and from the little I had heard from Johnny and others, was not sure I wanted to. Sounded like they would have no qualms at all about patching over.

Had never met them. Couple of weeks after returning from Buffalo, did get to see them though. When I least expected to.

(Information on biker gangs, their rules, regulations, history and customs and why they are called 1% ers can be found on 237)

(Information on a far more dangerous group of 1%ers can be found on 242)

CHAPTER 7

Poker was making me a decent wage by now, so I
gave up curb-siding. Had lots of time on my hands,
so I volunteered for a thrift store that raised funds
for a cat sanctuary. I'm more of a dog person, but
cats get a pretty raw deal from a lot of people and
are treated like disposable pets, so was a pleasure to
help where I could.

Things were slow in the store , and I was sitting at
the counter, staring out the window. I watched a cop
walk by my motorcycle, checking it out big time.
Two minutes later, he walked by again....then again
a minute after that. The bike was legal and I was in
no trouble that I knew of, so I decided to find out
what was going on. I walked out to the bike,
pretended to adjust the gas cock, then walked back
into the store. The cop was right on my ass.

"THAT YOUR BIKE?" He barked.

I nodded assent.

"LICENSE, OWNERSHIP AND
INSURANCE...NOW! " I almost expected him to
pull his gun and tell me to hit the floor he sounded
so angry.

I gave him what he asked for without saying a word.

"THIS IS NOT THE OWNERSHIP FOR THAT BIKE! THIS IS AN OWNERSHIP FOR A YAMAHA! THAT SAYS HARLEY DAVIDSON ON THE TANK! "

"Noooooo, it says Hardly Davidson's .....my idea of a joke. The bike is a Yamaha. I can't afford a Harley."

The face that had been white with anger started to turn crimson. He stared at the bike, then turned to me, mouth open, speechless for a few seconds.

"Oh." I could barely hear him now. " I got a call on my radio saying 'The Evil Ones' were coming my way, and I am all by myself here. I thought you were with them."

"Think you will find they don't drive Hardly's, and they sure as hell don't volunteer to help in charity thrift stores."

He mumbled something else, and left as fast as he had entered. Sure I saw beads of sweat forming on his brow.

Two minutes later, they rumbled by. Thirty of them in perfect formation, fifteen rows of two, no more than a few inches between the rear wheel of one bike and the front one of the next. It was as if they were one organism. And, an aptly named one at that. Evil looking. Once again I felt that strange chill I had felt at the age of fourteen. Cars pulled out of their way. Now I could empathize with that cop. Not a group you would want to confront on your own. Just behind the group with 'colours' on their back was a group of four more bikers, with what are known as 'bottom rockers' only. Bottom rockers are the the lower patch which shows the motorcycle club's location. I was not that surprised to see that one of them was Johnny. Looked like he was now what is known as a prospect with the Evil ones. Working towards becoming a 'full patch' member. He did not see me. I did not wave.

I saw that cop around a couple of times after that. He recognized me. He would always colour up, and grin sheepishly. I always smiled back. He never came into the store again though.

I worked at the thrift store for nothing. It was an all volunteer charity and I really admired the work they were doing. I worked at the gym a few hours a week too, on the weekend to give the owner a break. That I got paid for. I did not really need the money....I was doing just fine playing poker..... but it gave me a chance to get to know some of the members. Funny thing about true muscle head gyms. Everyone usually gets along with everyone else. Unlike your typical gym which usually have about a 50 50 male/female split, muscle head gyms are almost always exclusively male. They are the hang out of guys who really want to work out seriously, and as long as you go there to do that, nothing else much matters. Most of the guys that went to the gym were like the majority of members in gyms worldwide.

Gyms make their money from them. The type that joins for a few weeks, goes gung ho for a while, then gradually loses interest and stop coming. Funny thing is, when their membership expires, many of them come back and repeat the process. If everyone that belonged to a gym stuck it out there would never be room to move! At the other end of the scale were the hard core. Gyms make money from them too. That's because they get results from their hard work, and give the majority something to aim for, even if they will never make it. They keep coming back, basically two weeks on, fifty off, and that pays the bills. Being hard core myself, the hard core element were the guys who I tend to know the best.

One of my favourites was a guy by the name of Damion. You could not call Damion hard core really, although he was there a lot. Had a sort of girlish build. Tried hard but never seemed to put on much muscle. Damion was gay. Now, there's a funny word for you. I looked up why homosexuals are called gay. Gay came into use in the English language around about the 12th century, coming from the French word 'gai' Meaning joyful. That would fit Damion. Loved to laugh and make others laugh. Around about the 17th century it had become to also mean "addicted to pleasures and dissipation's" Couple of centuries later, the term 'gay man' meant a man that had sex with lots of women. Come the early 20th century, it started to also apply to men who had sex with lots of other men. Women could also be called gay....but that inferred they were prostitutes. Little sexual discrimination there. Seems it was in the early part of the 20th century that the gay men of the time...the ones having sex with other men.... pushed to have the term apply strictly to them, to avoid the word homosexual, which sounded like a disorder. They liked the term gay, and took it over. I told Damion I had looked it up, and what I had found out, and his quick response was:

"Can't say I like that part about gays having sex with lots of women! Eeeeew! Can't help but say the whole thing sounds a little queer to me ...... bummer." Typical Damion.

Damion always worked out with Jeffrey, a muscular guy that had a body odour problem. Nobody else would work out with him. Damion, who was always clean, seemed to enjoy the odour, along with Jeffery's tough way of dressing with leathers and chains and a peculiar old style pork pie hat. Different strokes for different folks. They made a peculiar couple, Damion at around 140 lbs and clean, Jeffrey at about 220 lbs and ugly as sin. We figured they were a couple outside the gym also, but that was their business. Ever noticed that gays with a name that can be shortened always seem to use the long version? Never Bob, or Jack or Jeff. I did not have too much to do with Jeffrey..... not because he was gay; unless you had a really bad cold, getting close was an uncomfortable experience. Always had a few words with Damion though. Nice guy.

Derek was a huge black guy. Must have weighed in

at around 260 lbs. Couple of inches shorter than me, but built like a tank. All muscle. Huge round head, shaved bald. The owner of the gym used to economize in the winter, keeping the temperature down to about 40 degrees....just enough to stop the pipes bursting. When Derek worked out in the winter, you could actually see steam rising from that cannonball of a head. Derek hardly spoke to anyone. When he did, it was in a surprising refined accent... but few noticed. Most people assumed he was poor because he was black, and because of his worn work out clothes. I liked him. We went out for a beer a few times after a workout, and only then did I find out he came from one of the wealthiest families in the area! He had been adopted at a very young age, had attended some of the best schools, and was working his way up in his dad's business. His brain was as big as the rest of him.

Derek and I could never become strong friends. We grew up in different worlds, totally alien to each other. He had been surrounded by wealth, I by poverty. But, in the gym we were equals. We what they call 'spotted' each other, making sure the heavy weights we used did not get out of control. When you are bench-pressing around 500 lbs, dropping that much weight down to your chest and then hoisting it back up again, you want to be sure you have someone that knows what they are doing in case something goes wrong. Once, back in Hardrock ,I had been trying to bench 400 lbs. for the first time. Could not quite do it...but that is how you get big: attempting what you cannot do, until you can. I had some young guy spot me. I got the weight down to my chest and was on the way back up when it got stuck. I just could not move it those last few inches. The thing to do if that happens and you are spotting, is to put one or two fingers under the bar and help just enough to break the sticking point. This guy panicked. God knows what he was thinking...if he was thinking at all. All I heard was "oh dear" and he reached out and hit the bar on one end! There I was with 400 lbs over me, with the bar swinging from side to side as I fought to control it. Adding to the problem was the fact that we are talking 'free weights' here. Nothing to hold them on the bar.....if one of those 45 lb weights came off, I would have an uneven weight to deal with, and almost certain serious injury. I could hear the guy saying "oh, oh" over and over. That was not helping much. Fear kicked in, and an adrenalin surge helped me get the bar under control and back on the supports.

The "oh, oh" was replaced with a chorus of "Oh, I'm sorry" Over and over. I just headed for the showers after telling him "shit happens." Few years back I would probably have hit the guy for being so incredibly stupid..... but I realized he had not meant any harm. For six months my back was in a painful spasm. I worked around it, using light weights Then, one day it felt as if someone had touched the painful part of my spine with a lit cigarette. Excruciating white hot pain for a few seconds, then the spasm disappeared as if it had never been. I always reckoned I must have pinched a nerve in my spine somehow, and it had freed itself in the end. Never did see a doctor, so don't know for sure. I knew a doctor would have said stop working out, and I was not prepared to do that. Do know that the very next time I tried 400 lbs, it went up no problem! In a sense that guy had helped me. Helped me get over what was probably a psychological barrier. I learned from that.

I could rely on Derek to spot me right. Derek was a guy I could rely on , in everything. Solid in every sense of the word. He actually offered me a chance to join his dad's company once, promising me a way of life that I would never have thought possible. That life suited Derek... he was bred for it. It was not for me. He understood. Instead, he introduced me to some of his dad's buddies who loved to play poker. Only stipulation was I could not play in the big games his dad played in. He had heard that I seldom lost and did not want his dad subjected to that. I taught the guys I played with how the game was really played, and they paid heavily for the lessons ... but it never seemed to bother them. They enjoyed the games, even though they never won. What I was winning was big time for me. To them it was chump change. True to my word I never attended a game where his dad was playing. I gathered from what I heard the pots got huge in some of those games, so I told them I was scared of such big stakes. They believed me. What can I say. I lie convincingly. I have a poker face.

Danny was another hard core who was OK to get

along with on a strictly casual basis....but you better count your fingers if you shook hands with him. Strange guy. He was a Gypsy. Think he took the reputation of Gypsies to heart and felt he had to live down to peoples expectations . Danny would rather make a dollar dishonestly than five fair and square.... and it was nothing to do with the effort involved. Just his nature. If you wanted anything that had 'fallen off a truck' Danny was your guy. He was one of Johnny's biggest customers. Took massive doses of steroids, and had a massively developed upper body. Never worked his legs. Considered himself a ladies man, and women obviously found his looks and attitudes to life attractive. If you met him outside the gym, always had a different pretty girl on his arm. Part of that may have been due to his skin though. Danny had an allergic reaction to steroids. Fortunately for him his face stayed relatively clear.... but the rest of him, where his skin was abraded by fabric, he developed huge boils. Did not stop him from using, but would think it turned a lot of women off when they saw him naked. Made us reluctant to use a bench after Danny had used it too. I always made sure there were bottles of disinfectant around to wipe down benches, and made damn sure I used them thoroughly before I worked out. Most of the other guys did too

Another guy most people had to look out for was Vito. Vito owed me his life. That is a story that would take a book to cover. Perhaps I'll write it sometime. Vito was the type of man that never forgot a slight, never forgot a favour. Saving a man's life is about as big a favour as you can give him, so as far as Vito was concerned he would always owe me. He'd found me a couple of poker games where I was always welcome. I think Vito was 'connected', though we never discussed it. I never would have gotten into those games without him. I never would have survived those games, if the other guys didn't know I was tight with Vito. We would never be friends, but I knew I could count on him without question.

Tim was I guy I got to meet only briefly, but will mention for interest. Didn't particularly like him as he was a bit of a show off and a braggart. Always talking about his success with the ladies and always flashing a wad of cash. But, I did not have to socialize with him outside the gym, so you roll with the punches. He asked me once what I thought of steroids. I told him that steroid use can cause heart and liver damage, cause fatty deposits to develop on the pectorals (bitch tits), cause severe mood swings ('roid rage) , lead to muscle tears, and can even cause impotence in some men. Other than that they were OK. I don't want to mess with anything that can destroy one of the major 'muscles' a man has . Way I said it was I don't mess with anything that may mess with my pecker. Not too struck on the other possibilities either. He just laughed. Told me he had been using them long before I knew him and sure was not going to stop. Said there was nothing wrong with his pecker. I just smiled and reminded him he had asked for my opinion. I'd given it to him.

One day not long after that, I was spotting him on a bench press. The man was obsessed with his pecs...gym slang for pectoral muscles. He used to brag that women said they saw his chest enter the room before he did. Personally I have found that most women are not that impressed with big chests the way men are on women.. I had seen some of the women he went out with , and was fairly certain that a big fat bulge in a man's pants was far more important to them. Not the obvious bulge you probably think I'm talking about, the bulge a fat wallet full of money makes in a back pocket. But, not for me to say. Tim hoisted the weights off the bar. Later, he told me it 'felt funny' but could not explain why. He dropped the weight hard and fast towards his chest, and I watched his chest muscle tear off in waves. I was not expecting that. I would have thought any damage would occur on the way back up when you are struggling and straining against the weight. Nope. The tearing happens on the way down. He was lucky. I have fast reflexes, and took most of the weight before it hit his chest..... but a lot of damage had already been done. At the time, he did not feel any pain. But, I knew he had done serious damage, and I drove him to Emergency. Pain started about when we got there. Guess shock masked it for a while. I would have stayed with him, but had to drop him off and get back to the gym... I was the only one on duty. Next day he came in to thank me. He was obviously upset, but he started to laugh anyway. I asked him what was so funny.

"Dave, I've got to tell you. I've been remembering that little lecture you gave me on steroids. I walked into Emergency, and it was full, as usual. I went up to the desk and told them I had torn my pec. off. The nurse gave me a funny look, eyed me up and down, and told me to have a seat. I waited 3 hours to see a doctor, watched everyone else go in before me. Pain was getting worse by the hour. In the end, I went back up. Different nurse. Pointed to my pec and told her it really hurt where I had torn it off. She looked at me funny too. Saw she was suppressing a smile. Then she said

"I'm so sorry sir. The other nurse thought you said you had torn your pecker off.... and she could not see any blood. We thought you had a mental problem. I'll get someone to see you now."

I felt sorry for him, but had to laugh along with him. I know he had it sown back on, but he never came back into the gym. Often wonder if he gave up steroids. Obvious bad for the pecker *and* the pecs.

Then, there was Johnny. Johnny was a member of the gym, but we hardly ever saw each other any more. He came into the gym a few times a month, but usually in the evenings when I was not there. Gathered he belonged to most of the gyms in town, and worked out in them all. Gave him a chance to sell his wares.

Then he came in one Saturday morning. He was obviously doing well. He was now driving a gorgeous chopped Harley and always had a huge wad of cash on him. Was obviously using as well. It takes years and years to build up muscle honestly....but every time we met he seemed bigger. It had been about six months since I had seen him last. Guess such 'impressive' gains were good for business. Advertising for his products. He was short and slim by nature, but the juice was making up for that. I did not like the changes I saw in him, neither the puffy look of steroids, or the changes in his personality. It was not that good to start with as far as I was concerned, and was deteriorating fast. I guess the feeling was mutual. He and I were going in different directions, and we both knew it.

I basically ignored him while he worked out, and he chatted to members who were obviously his customers. When he had finished his work out and his business transactions, he came over and spoke to me.

"What the fuck you doing working in here for minimum wage Paladin? We could use a guy with your muscle. We're getting into offering protection to local businesses. Easy money. Few hundred bucks from each business we protect. Nothing to it. All you have to do is call around and collect. Hardly ever have to bust anyone up."

"I do this 'cause I like it Johnny. You know my main source of income is on the tables. I take money from people who have a choice to gamble, or not. No way I'd take money from some poor working stiff trying to make a living. Know how hard that can be."

"It don't have to be hard at all. I could help you make major dollars. Your trouble is your way too fucking soft. Way too fucking soft. Told you that when I gave you that name. In this world you take what you can. Survival of the fittest. Sooner you learn that the better. Mark my words."

I just smiled , said nothing, watched him walk out, jump on his Harley, peel off. I knew the 'we' he had mentioned were 'The Evil Ones'. I understood why guys like the ones I grew up with rebelled against a world that rejected them. But in almost all things in this life you have to be careful not to let the pendulum swing too far. 1% ers as a group were bad news as far as I was concerned.... and The Evil Ones were right up there with the worst of them. More I heard about them, the less I liked them. More Johnny was with them, the more of it rubbed off on him. Just because I understood more than most why they became the way they did, did not mean I had to hang out with them. But, it seems we were destined to meet.

CHAPTER 8

Fate. Destiny. Life. Is it preordained? I don't think so..... but who knows? Certainly not the ones that tell you they do. As Buckminster Fuller said, "The Universe is a locked safe, with the combination inside." But we cant help but think about it. Personally, I do think some things in the future are destined to be. How we are affected by them is sometimes up to us, and sometimes up to things we do not understand. There is a LOT in this world that is impossible for us to understand, and understanding that is sometimes one of the hardest things of all.

My grandfather was a huge man. My dad and I take after him. When World War 11 broke out he was a stoker on steam locomotives in England. With a massive build and a stubborn nature, he was one of the best they had. Could shovel coal into the fires for twelve hours straight, and was used on the fastest trains, often the Flying Scott between London and Glasgow . Fast trains became an essential service, and the men that could feed them coal became essential as well : bombs, munitions and supplies needed to be transported around the country in a hurry. So, while other guys went off to flog their way through the mud of Europe, he shuttled trains back and forth across England at a rate that would kill most men. My grandmother tells me he would come home sometimes so tired he would fall asleep in a chair with a cup of tea in his hand. His body craved salt so much food would be covered in amounts that would make most people gag. To light a cigarette he could reach into a fire, pull out a burning ember from the edge of the fire, light it and toss the coal back, his hands were so callused from shovelling coal. Gentle by nature, his mind and body were as tough as the steel that his shovel was made from. He faced anything, anyone, head on.

Well, almost anything. Trains and train stations were obvious targets for German bombers. That was just an accepted part of the job. He made it through the war.... but he shouldn't have.

Usually he came back exhausted, and slept the sleep of the dead. Then, all of a sudden he started having nightmares. Every night the same thing. Every night he woke up in a sweat. In his nightmares one of the stations he was working out of was bombed before the train could leave the station. These nightmares continued for a week.... until it was the day he was supposed to report to that particular station. My grandmother convinced him to do something he had never done before.... call in sick. You guessed it.... the station was bombed. You can call it coincidence. I think not, preferring to believe it is related to the feeling I get when I meet a psychopath. Just one of the things we don't understand. Different folks have different strengths and weaknesses. This feeling I get in the presence of psychopaths I feel is related to what my grandfather had. I thank my grandfather for that. It had warned me of their presence several times. It was about to do it again.

It had now been a couple of years since I had seen Johnny. He wasn't coming in that often, and I only worked a few hours a week at the gym, six hours Saturday morning. Then, there he was. At opening time, 6am. I had never known him to be up that early. It took a few seconds to recognize him. His face had that puffy look heavy steroid users get, and his arms were twice the size they had been only a couple of years ago. They were bare, to allow the scabs to heal. Fresh scabs from heavy, jailhouse style tattoos. Jagged silver rings adorned every finger, the type most bad assed bikers wear. The type that will tear your face to pieces when they hit you. He had the typical LOVE tattoo on his left knuckles, HATE on his right. The rest were mostly geometric patterns covering from the wrists up to the delts, with two exceptions. On the right bicep he had The Evil One's logo, on the left , 1% er. Johnny was definitely one scary looking motherfucker.

Personally I have never understood tattoos. Don't like them, and don't feel the need to look tough. I avoid trouble when I can and don't need to look tough when I can't. I reckoned that many fresh tattoos must hurt, but said nothing. For Johnny to make the effort to come in at 6 am, he must want to talk. I'd let him. I just smiled, nodded, and waited for him to say what was on his mind.

"Paladin, my man! Long time no see! But, I was talking about you last night."

I waited.

"I was talking to Nails about you man. He really wants to meet you!"

"Who the fuck is 'Nails' Johnny?" I reckoned it had to be one of his new friends. I had never heard of him, but it sure sounded like the type of name a biker would use. I was thinking it sounded a little effeminate... as I had images of manicured fingers dancing in my brain, but kept that thought to myself. I did not think Johnny would find that funny these days, although he would have just a few years ago. I reckoned it was "Nails' as in 'tough as'.

"Nails is president of the Evil Ones. Real smart dude. Real smart. Real good dude to know. Me and him have become real tight. I've been in the joint for the last little while and got to know him there. We just got out a month or so ago. I'm making mountains of bread because of him. Him and I were talking about poker last night. Told him you were the best player there ever was. He has an idea for making really big bucks. Want's to meet you. You've got to meet him. He was in the pen for a six year stretch, and says he want to make up for lost time. Spent his time in the can thinking out ways to make money...and fuck me Johnny, I can tell you he is really good at it. Got that Hog I'm riding because of him, and just bought me a really nice set of wheels...

a totally restored 1960 T Bird convertible. White with red leather. 352 motor. You'll cream your draws when you see it Paladin. Cost 50 grand. Paid cash. All because of him. Real nice guy. You'll love him."

I seriously doubted that. Was beginning to realize I did not like Johnny that much any more.... and anyone that was president of a group like The Evil Ones did not sound like someone any sane person would want to meet. I should have told Johnny that there was no way. But, for old times sake, I hummed and hawed.

"Damn Johnny. You know I am not into joining clubs. I've always been a loner. Always will be. Besides. I do pretty good from poker all by myself. Why would I want to share that with someone?"

"Call me 'Bullwhip' Paladin. All my friends do these days. I ain't asking you to join nothing. Just want you to hear what he has to say. What are you making right now, 5 grand a month tops?"

I just smiled faintly and tilted my head. What I made was my business.

"Fuck, that's chump change. Nails will get you making serious bread man. All I'm asking is for you to listen to what he has to say. I've vouched for you, and he wants to meet. There is a big party up at the club house tonight. I really want you to come. You'll have a really good time, and you can hear what he has to say. Lots of chicks. It'll be like old times.

You'll be doing me a huge, huge favour. Helping him is good for me. It'll be good for you too. Guaranteed."

I seriously doubted that. I should have said no. I should have said I had a game. But, I didn't. I found myself nodding my head, for old times sake.

"Fuckin A Paladin, fuckin A! I'd pick you up in my T Bird, but we always take bikes out to the club house. Especially tonight. It's a big night for me. Big night. You still living in that same dump?"

I nodded.

"I'll swing by your place on my hog around nine. Have your bike polished. We'll ride up together."

Johnny did not wait for any reply. He flashed me a big grin, and turned around to leave. He'd had no intention of working out. He'd just come to see me. On his way out, he met Damion, and it appeared he deliberately shouldered him out of the way, almost knocking him to the floor. I had a real bad feeling about what I had just agreed to.

Damion stared as Johnny jumped on his Harley, a work of art that must have set him back 30 grand. Johnny peeled off without a second look back. Damion walked up to me.

"Going to have a serious hematoma where he bounced off me Johnny." Anyone else would have

said bruise.... but I knew that is what he meant.
"Don't think he likes people like me. Pity. I could
like him. Such a beeeautiful body, and such a
beeeautiful bike. Just love those tats. Mean devil
though. Hmmm. That remind me of a joke." Typical
Damion.

I smiled. After a bad start to the day, one of his jokes
would be a pleasant diversion.

"A man dies, and finds himself outside the gates of
hell. Instead of going in, he sits down and cries. The
next morning, he is still sitting there crying. The
devil saunters out to see what the problem is.
"What's the matter pal? Why so sad?"
"This is hell! HELL! I never expected to end up
here." He starts to wail afresh.
"Now come on pal, you were no saint on earth, were
you?"
The guy shakes his head. "No, but I never expected
to end up in hell."
"There, there. It's not so bad. Truth is, those pussies
up in heaven paint us a lot worse than what we are.
Tell me, did you drink on earth?"
The man wails some more. "Yes. I know I shouldn't
have. But, I had a hard life. I had to drink to take the
edge off"
The devil nods his head sympathetically. "I
understand. Believe me. But, think about it. All the
bootleggers, all the owners of distilleries, all the
brewers, they all end up here! Every last one of 'em,
We have the best of the best. And, Jesus...you will
excuse me, that is my favourite cuss word... we

don't care if you drink. In fact we encourage it. Every Monday, from the second you wake up until the last stroke of midnight, all we do is drink! The best there is of everything! And, you don't have to worry about sclerosis of the liver...you're dead!" The guy stopped crying. You could see him thinking.

"Did you smoke ?" asked the devil.

"Yes. Like I said, life was hard. Cigarettes helped me cope."

"Well, you don't seriously think any guy in the tobacco industry went to heaven do you? Jesus, we have them all ! We don't care if you smoke. Indeed, every Tuesday is dedicated to smoking . From the second you wake up until the last stroke of midnight, all we do is smoke! The best there is of everything! And, you don't have to worry about cancer ...you're dead!"

Now, the devil really had his attention.

"Come on now, be honest. Did you do drugs?"

"Yes.Yes I did."

"I knew it!! You know what I am going to tell you, don't you? All the dealers, all the pushers, they end up here! Every Wednesday , from the second you wake up until the last stroke of midnight, all we do is take drugs! The best there is of everything!God damn it, you don't have to worry about an overdose, ...you're dead!"

The guy actually started to smile. Got to his feet.

"OK. The biggie. Did you like sex?"

The guy nods his head enthusiastically.

"That's my boy. It's a big deal here...a big deal. In fact, we dedicate four days to sex! Thursdays,

Fridays, Saturdays, Sundays. We don't take Sundays off down here! From the second you wake up Thursday to the last stroke of midnight Sunday, all we do is have sex! You don't need Viagra.... everyone is always up for it And,God damn it, you don't have to worry about disease ...you're dead!"
The guy has a great big grin on his face. The devil puts his arm around his shoulder, smiles and leads him through the gates. As the gates close, the devil turns to the man.
"Oh, by the way, are you gay?"
The guy looks at him dumbfounded.
"Of course not!"
"Oh dear. I don't think you're going to like Thursday to Sunday much."

I could not help but roar with laughter.

"Enjoy your workout Damion. Look after that hematoma!" I would not have laughed if I knew it was the last time I would ever hear one of his jokes.

(For a selection of Damion's jokes, see page 234)

CHAPTER 9

Johnny came to my place at nine. I was waiting outside on my unwashed bike. If he thought I was going to spruce it up to make it look good, he had another thought coming. He did not stop. Just slowed down. I pulled in behind him. The trip through town was a little uncomfortable. I could sense the disapproval as we drove by people. Johnny seemed not to notice. Once we got outside of town it felt better. I realized we were on the same road that lead to Frank's diner. We turned off about two miles before we got to Frank's, and headed a few miles down a dark, deserted road. We pulled into their club house around 9:30. It was out in the country, far from any other building. Place looked like it was ready for a siege, big steel door, and windows covered in steel shutters with small slits in various locations, I assumed to allow guns to fire out. Paranoia is alive and flourishing in any outlaw motorcycle gang. We parked our bikes with the others. There had to be close to a million dollars worth of metal there. I had to admit my bike looked a little insignificant.

Inside, the place was jumping. It was a big building, just one huge room on the main floor. There were three interior doors, two made of steel all them off to the back of the building. One was open, and appeared to go to the basement. The other was locked. I assumed it went upstairs. I later found out it was the apartment given to the president. The third door, made of wood, was open. Beyond it I could see the most disgusting toilet I had ever seen. Black in it's entirety from some sort of fungus. No lid, crap and piss on the floor and even the walls. Boxes piled on one side, also covered in fungus and filth.

Bright lights made up for the lack of windows, and heavy metal music blasted from huge speakers. The air was thick with marijuana smoke and the smell of spilt beer. There were about 50 guys in the place, and, surprisingly, about 10 women. Some of them were not bad looking in a hard sort of way. They were what bikers called splashers, or patch snatch : girls that would have sex with any biker. The thought of having anything to do with a woman that would fuck or suck the guys I saw here was enough to shrivel my dick up as if it had been dipped in ice water. But, that's just me.

As we walked in the door a 350 lb beer barrel walked towards us. I'm six feet two...but this guy towered over me. That cold feeling down my spine hit me hard when he was still ten feet off. I did not have to be told that this was Nails. He certainly did not look as if he worked out, but I was sure he did. It was the kind of body that had no real defined muscles, but was as hard as a rock. His huge head was bald, and covered in scars. Looked like he'd been beaten over the head with iron bars. Found out later he had. He'd taken on a half dozen members of what was once called the Satan's Choice ,before they were patched over as Hells Angels. They had iron pipes. He had his fists. He'd won. His cold eyes looked jet black, like those of a stuffed animal, only far too evil for any toy. He had three tears tattooed below his right eye. Oh, and no manicure on those two huge hams he carried at the end of his arms. The only things adorning them were tattoos and rings similar to the ones Johnny wore, only twice as big to accommodate his huge fingers. Tattoos all over his arms, similar to Johnny's, and peeking out from under his T shirt. Looked like he had a full body suit of black ink. As well as tattoos on his arms, I noticed track marks. There was an unusual necklace of what looked like finger nails around his neck. A lot of them. I decided not to ask him what they were all about. His colours ...the jacket that 1% ers wear to proclaim to the world who they are.... was covered in what are known as patches. Some of them I recognized, some I did not. Bike clubs use patches much like the armed forces use medals, awarding them for things that they feel are worth noting. He had the Filthy Few patch, awarded for a murder or an extreme assault performed for the club, the Dequiallo patch awarded for fighting with law enforcement, and a full set of 'wings' ; patches awarded for various sex acts, ranging all the way from having sex with a virgin to having sex with a known carrier of venereal disease. Those were the patches I recognized from reading books. I didn't know what the others stood for. Didn't want to. This was a psycho who did not hide behind a winning smile.

"You must be Paladin" he yelled. " Come outside. Can't talk here."

Nails, Johnny and I stepped outside, closing the door to cut of the heavy metal din. I waited for them to talk. There were a couple of guys admiring each others bikes, but they kept their distance. I don't think Nails was the kind of guy to politely ask you to mind your business.

"Paladin" He said it with a sneer. "Kind of a sissy type name don't you think?" I did not tell him the image that had come to my mind when I heard he was called Nails. "We are gonna have to come up with a better name than that" He talked as if I was going to be seeing a lot of him. I said nothing. You are waaay prettier than I bargained on. But, that can be an advantage. Johnny tells me you are the best, and that's good enough for me. But that fucking rice burner your riding!" He looked over at my Yamaha. "That's an embarrassment! I'll get you a Hog. A gift." I just smiled. Like I said before, you can't insult me. Even if you could, I would not have reacted, and he knew it. You don't pick a fight with the 350 lb president of an outlaw motorcycle gang, especially on his home turf. Even if you can beat him, and I doubted I could. I was fast, and I was good, but that body of his would absorb a lot of punishment, and just one punch from those knuckle dusters he and Johnny wore would finished the fight. Even if by some miracle I managed to get the best of him, I would be a dead man walking. Outlaw bikers live by the code of one for all and all for one.

You pick a fight with any full patch member and you've picked a fight with them all. All at once. My mother didn't have any stupid kids.

"The Hog will be a gift. I'll get you a nice one. Then I've got plans that will make you very wealthy indeed. I've had my eye on a really wealthy old Jew."

Ever notice how people with extreme prejudices just assume you share them? The way he said Jew sounded like the worst sort of obscenity. Anybody else, anywhere else, I would have had to say I was Jewish. I'm not, but I don't like prejudiced pricks. Anyone else, I would have loved to see them squirm. But, like I said, my mother didn't have any stupid kids. I kept quiet. " Big bucks brought to those games of his. I want to hit one of them. I want you inside. I'll stake you. You keep your winnings. No one will know. When I hit the games your money will disappear just like theirs..... but I'll give it back to you. Trust me. Then I have a couple of other games in other cities I want to hit. Can't overdo it. I wont put you at risk." I almost smiled. I thought he was going to say 'trust me' again. "The heists locally are just warm ups. Then I have really big plans for you. Trust me" There it was again. "Gonna make you a really wealthy man. Gonna be fun. No worries. You just ask your old pal Bullwhip here. "

He looked at Johnny and Johnny looked at me, bobbing his head like one of those bubble head dolls. I reckoned Nails wasn't used to taking no for an answer, and I reckoned he thought I had dollar bills floating in front of my eyes. I wasn't going to give him the answer he wanted, but I wasn't going to piss him off either. I reckoned if I handled this wrong my mother wouldn't have any kids at all. I wanted to tell him to fuck off. Instead I said:

"Fuck Nails. I could sure use the money. But, I have to think about it for a couple of days. I can handle the job no problem. No one would ever know I was working with you. That's what a poker face is all about. But, I sure don't want to end up in the can. Tempting offer ....but I have to think."

"Understandable Paladin. Take a day or so. I'm sure you will see it my way. And, don't worry. I would never let you down. I've been in the pen for the last 6 years. Would never do anything to send you there or me back. Never! No risk involved. Trust me." There it was again. "But, right now, it is partay time!! Everything is on me. Pick any girl you want, tell her I said it was OK. All the booze is free. We have the best. All the drugs...anything you want... all free. Enjoy. Learn to live like an Evil One! Learn what it is like to be one of the boys. Right now, me and the boys have important business to discuss. Enjoy!"

I was reminded of Damion's joke. I thought of asking if there was any gay sex.... but then I thought twice.

"Stick around. The meeting will take about an hour

or so. Then we are going to play chicken snatch. Usually, just full patch members can play. But, I'll let you in. First prize is key of coke. I just made a big score." For the first time, he actually smiled at me. It was not a pretty sight. Think I was supposed to be impressed, and excited about the chance to win about $20,000 worth of cocaine. He handed me his card. The ass hole actually had cards printed up that just said Nails, with a phone number.

The idea of handing out cards began with the Frisco Hells Angels back in the 60's. They used to hand out a card every time they helped a stranded motorist. On one side, the card said "You Have Been Assisted by a Member of the Hells Angels, Frisco". On the reverse they said "When we do right no one remembers. When we do wrong, no one forgets." But, so many stranded motorists were freaking out when what to them looked like a creature from another planet stopped to give them help, the idea faded away. The idea of Nails ever helping anyone but himself was almost enough to make me burst out laughing.

"Keep the card, Paladin. Call me when you have had time to think things through. Time to partay!"

We went back inside. The heavy metal was as loud as ever. Nails didn't bother to speak. He just looked around the room and headed for the basement. All the full patch members reacted as if on cue. One guy was actually in the process of getting a blow job from one of the splashers. He just turned around and followed the others, a grin on his face, zipping himself up as he walked. The girl was left sucking wind, so to speak. It didn't seem to bother her. Took it as if it was a natural occurrence. I noticed that Johnny followed, even though he was not a full patch member. There were five other guys left with me upstairs. I guessed they had been invited for various reasons. There wasn't one of them that would not have scared the bejesus out of any normal citizen. I reckoned that made two girls for every guy, 'cause I sure as hell was not staying around. I waited 'till the last full patch member disappeared downstairs, closing the door behind him. It was blow job guy. Guess it's hard to walk that way without getting yourself all tied up in your zipper. One of the other invited guests yelled over to him "Don't you worry Snake, I'll let her finish off on me!" Snake grinned. I stepped outside. Nothing in there I wanted. I resisted the urge to kick all the other bikes over, jumped on my Hardly and went home. I did not sleep well that night. Lots to think about. I did not get to sleep until about 4 am

CHAPTER 9

I was awoken around 11 am by a banging on my door. It was Johnny. He did not look pleased. I sleep in the nude, and answered the door that way. Johnny was reminded that at 6'1" and 230 lbs, I am cut to ribbons.... no fat. And, I know he was remembering how fast I was when I wanted to be. His pupils were a little dilated. Behind his pupils, I could see his brain ticking over. Finally, he spoke.

"Get dressed Paladin. I'll take you for a ride in my T Bird. We can go to breakfast like old times. We have to talk. He smiled. I did not. I did meet him downstairs ten minutes later though. I had some questions I needed answering. I had decided I really did not give a shit about what he wanted to talk about. There was nothing about this man I wanted anything to do with. I did have to agree that his T Bird was one of the nicest I had ever seen. Looked better than it had when it drove off the sales floor back in 1960. I did not say that though. I just got in, didn't say a word. He drove off. I waited for him to talk. It took a while.

"I'm trying to keep my cool here Paladin. I'm still coming down from yesterday. If I wander a bit in my conversation, you have to understand. I dropped acid for the first time last night at the meeting. Fantastic fucking high, but it's taking me a while to get my head straight here. I'm trying to understand why the fuck you took off last night before we finished out meeting. I 'struck' with the Evil Ones last night. Became full patch! Acid was part of the celebration. Big night for me. I told you it was going to be special for me. I'm full patch now Paladin. That's a big deal! You disappointed me man, and Nails was really pissed."

I wanted to tell him that I wanted nothing to do with him or his new found buddies. Wanted to tell him that they could all go to hell...indeed was certain they would if there was such a place. But, I also wanted some answers of my own, and I wanted to figure a way for me to get out of this mess, so I kept my cool. Saying what I actually thought could get me killed. Not by Johnny. I could handle him. But I knew death was waiting for me just around the corner, waiting for me to take a wrong step.

"Sorry if I caused you aggro, and upset Nails, but I needed to think about what he had proposed. Had to get out of there to do that. Important decisions can't be made if you are stoned." I wanted to add 'you dumb fuck' but bit my tongue. "Glad I had the time to think, cause I have a lot of questions, and I aint making a decision till I have the answers. You can supply those answers." My first question really should have been: 'what made you think I would be interested in being used by Nails?' Instead, I asked questions that I figured would confirm my uneasy suspicions.

" First you can tell me what those tear tattoos on his face are all about, what that strange necklace is all about, what the hell a man you say I can trust is doing with fresh track marks on his arm, and what the fuck is a chicken snatch?"

Johnny looked at me as if he could not understand the relevance of the questions. I could understand that. They had no relevance to his agenda. But, they did with mine.

"The tears? He got those in the pen. They can have lots of meanings. Can mean you have been raped while inside...can you imagine anyone trying to rape Nails?" Johnny smiled for the first time. He seemed to think that was funny. "Can just be a kind of badge of honour to say you have been in the pen. Nails don't need to brag about that" He smiled again. "The most common meaning is you have killed someone." Nails says he had three put on 'cause he thought that looked cool. Said in fact, if he had a tear for everyone he had iced, he'd have teardrops down to the end of his dick!" He smiled again.

"The necklace. That is more serious business. It's how he got his name. Nails got sent to the pen for running girls. They could not pin everything on him, but enough to give him a six year stretch. Apparently the guys would pick up girls fresh into town.... dumb farm chicks looking for excitement. They would bring them back to the club, and as the president, he broke them in. He 'nailed em' two ways. First he fucked the daylights out of them.

Then he kept them there for a few weeks while all the guys had their fun. By the end of two weeks, all the fight was fucked out of them. Then he told them they belonged to the club and they were going to earn money on the streets. If they did not do what they were told, he would find them, wherever they were, and kill them. To make sure they realized he was serious, he pulled out the fingernail on their little finger, and added it to his necklace. I gather it worked real well as a deterrent." I could see Johnny thought this was smart...could see the hint of a smile on his lips. I wanted to kill him right there, but said nothing, showed no emotion.

"The track marks? Nails loves heroin. Says he needs it to relax. But, you have nothing to worry about. He can handle it. Don't worry, he thinks things through better than anyone I ever met. Real sharp dude. He does not let the smack get in the way of business. He's solid. Would never let you down, put you in harms way. You have his word and mine. Take it to the bank." If I had not been so white hot boiling mad, it would have been my time to smile. To laugh out loud actually. I just sat there, staring at Johnny.

"Now, the chicken snatch. That might bother you some, knowing how you feel about animals. But it shouldn't. Chickens are stupid, and they have a shitty life anyway. Don't get mad now, but what the chicken snatch is sounds worse than it is. If you had been there, you would see it was exciting. Those chickens die fighting for their lives. Gotta be better than sitting in a cage all their lives unable to move, right? Nails releases a half dozen chickens and everyone chases after them, trying to catch 'em, trying to tear a piece off 'em. . The guy that ends up with the largest piece of chicken wins. Them birds are dumb man. They sure fight for their lives.... but do you know they still run around after their heads have been torn off ? That is if they have legs left."

He was looking at me as he said all this, just occasionally flicking a look to the road. I knew he was going to smile, and I knew I was going to punch him in the face, and to hell with the consequences. But, before I could punch his lights out, somebody turned all the lights out. They should not have gone out. It was daytime.

You ever notice in the movies how people drive while having a conversation and hardly ever look at the road? Bad idea. A lot can happen on the road in a fraction of a second, and those movie guys look away for seconds at a time.

When the lights came back on, I was on the pavement. Wet stuff was running down the side of my face. The front of shirt had changed colour. It had been blue. Now it was a dark reddish black. A few people were standing around me, staring. I thought that was rude. When I stood up, they left me and went over to the larger crowd near Johnny. Johnny was sitting in the drivers seat of his car, snoring slowly and loudly. I thought that was odd. He had been awake a few seconds ago. That was odd too. The metal support of the sun visor was stuck in the side of his head. It should not have been there...The lights went out again.

Only time in my life I get to ride in an ambulance, and I miss it. I don't know if I stayed out cold on my own accord, or whether they helped me to. No one ever told me. It was a busy time at the hospital that day.

At the scene, I gather they initially thought the accident was our fault. Johnny was 'known' to the police, and empty beer cans had come flying out of the back of the car upon impact. Guess drinking and driving wasn't a problem for Johnny....but he had not been doing it then. Looked like drunk driving to the cops. Ironically, they guy that hit us should have been 'known' to the police also. He was one himself ! An off duty cop. Turned out he had hit several cars a mile or so away, seriously hurting some of the people in the cars, and almost taking the arm off a young girl walking with her mother on the sidewalk. He hit them getting away from the cars he had hit. Gather he tore off from there. Think he had slowed down quite a lot by the time he met us coming the other way, or we would have been dead. I reckon he was looking over his shoulder to see if he was being followed, and veered over into our path. To be fair to Johnny, I don't think it would have made any difference if he had been watching where he was going. Neither Johnny or I stank of booze, but that off duty cop sure did.

I heard all this while I was laying in emergency,

listening to the nurses. I was the very least of their problems. Turned out I had a nasty cut in my scalp that bled profusely, but was not deep or dangerous. And I had a concussion, which did not seem to be too bad. Every once in a while one of the nurses would come over and ask me a question to see if I was clear headed. I was. I asked my own questions in return and they filled in where they could. 1960 T Birds do not have shoulder seat belts, and we were not wearing the lap belts it did have . Stupid I know, but there you go. Because I am so tall, I was lucky. Instead of hitting the side post or the windshield, I had gone over the top. They reckon I scrapped skin off my scalp when I hit the sidewalk. Must have been a glancing connection with the pavement, cause it was not serious. My shoulder ached like a son of a bitch and the skin was messed up there too, but nothing was broken. Johnny was not so lucky. He had whacked into the post, and somehow the metal bar that was inside the sun visor had lodged in his head. He was not in the emergency room. He was in emergency surgery and was in serious condition. The young girl was in surgery also as the doctor's saved her arm. The rest of us were in the emergency ward. I was by far and away the least of their problems.

After a few hours, I asked if I could go home. It was a busy, busy day, so they had no objections. I was told to come back to be checked in a few days. I never did. They were nice enough to get someone to drive me home. They had given me some pain killers. My head hurt like hell. I took a couple and crashed.

Now, you would think that off duty cop would have had the book thrown at him, right? Uh uh.
Cops stick by their own amazingly similarly to the way motorcycle 1%ers stick by their own. When emergency staff reported the smell of alcohol on him not us, their lawyer claimed he had his first ever acute diabetic emergency! The lawyer knew that diabetic ketoacidosis causes the body to try and remove ketones from the body via the mouth and makes a person smell like a distillery. You can believe that's what happened if you like. I don't think so. I don't know if they got away with that or not. Would not surprise me. Have heard of far more far fetched excuses being used to get them out of tight jambs. As you'll hear, I was long gone when it all settled. No one ever tried to contact me, and I never bothered to find out. Think you can take it to the bank that the lawyers story held up.

CHAPTER 10

Next morning I woke up and did not feel too bad. I took it easy around the apartment, reading and thinking. Mostly thinking. Following morning was another story. I woke up blind.

That is a scary feeling! I knew I was awake, and I knew I had opened my eyes.... but I could not see a thing. Then, a glimmer of light came in. Then I could see in front of me as if looking through a crack. I went to the bathroom and had to laugh....partly from relief, partly because I looked so funny. I had what they call deep bruising... or deep hematomas as Damion would say. Looked like I had gone a couple of rounds with the heavyweight champion of the world with my hands tied behind my back. Two magnificent black eyes, Black triangles below each eye, with the pointed end of the triangle reaching all the way down to the top of my mouth. I spent that day with a bag of frozen peas pressed to my face. Ten minutes on, ten minutes off and back in the freezer. Luckily, I had lots to think about to keep me busy. Slept OK that night, and woke up able to see, no problem. Repeated the process. The following morning, my eyes popped wide open and I was scared in a way I had never been in my life before.

Not too much scares me. What I saw that morning

did. I woke up and and moved up on my elbows from the bed. Open my eyes, then had them forced wide open. My cupboard door was ajar, and sitting on top of the door were two of the most hideous creatures to ever grace a nightmare. Only this was no nightmare. I was awake. No words could describe them. Up to then, I had never seen a gargoyle, but when I saw some later in life, I knew what had inspired them...although even the ugliest never came close to the things I saw. I have seen some ugly bastards in my life, seen eyes on some of them that would intimidate the bravest soul....but nothing close to the evil and hate in those eyes. Later in life, after seeing gargoyles for the first time, I looked up where they came from. Historians speculate that people in the middle ages were inspired to create them after finding the remains of dinosaurs. I don't think so! Whatever the hell I saw, they saw too. I only saw them for a second, and then they gradually dissolved, right in front of my eyes. Never seen anything like it before or since. Never want to. I have since met only one other person that has seen them. You'll meet him later. Unless you have seen a similar thing, you'll think I was either still asleep, or hallucinating. I was not. Or, you'll think it was an extreme reaction to what I was planning. Sorry. Not a chance. I had no second thoughts about what I was planning, and have no regrets to this day. Could be you'll think I am nuts. You could be right....but then we all are in some way or other. We all have our own brand of crazy. That ain't mine. Don't really care too much if you believe me or not. I know what I saw. Wish I hadn't. But, they did not drive me to take up religion, and they did not make me change my mind about what I had to do. So, think what you like. I did not sleep well the next night..... but never saw them again.

Next day was Saturday. My day to work in the gym. 6 am I opened up. As usual, Derek was the first one in. During the week he came in at 6 so he could be at his desk by 8. Kept the same routine on the weekends. He was concerned when he first saw me, but when I assured him I was OK, first thing he did was laugh at my face. Said he was sorry, but he could not help it. Asked me if I was trying to turn black. Said he did not recommend it.....did not think I would get lucky like him and be adopted by a wealthy family. Told me I had the colour just right though....I obviously had an 'eye' for such things. Indeed, two eyes. We kidded back and forth, then I got serious. I told him what Nails had said. I knew Derek's parents were Jewish, and was pretty certain I knew who he had been talking about. Told him no way I would be taking up the offer, but thought he should know what the psycho was planning. He thanked me profusely and said he would make sure that any poker game his dad was in was protected. Then he went for his work out. We joked again on his way out, and it was as if I had said nothing. But I knew Derek. Extremely efficient. I pitied anyone that tried one on with his family.

Damion was usually next in, but he was a no show. Thought to myself, Damn. I could use a joke or two right now.

Vito came in next. He was concerned. Figured someone had taken a baseball bat to me. I told them that if they had, he would have read about it in the papers.... they would have been dead. He laughed and told me anytime I needed anything...anything, all I had to do was ask Any problem, he would look after it for me. I told him I could look after my own problems, but did have some favours to ask. Never seen him so happy. This man had a deeply ingrained sense of honour, and I knew it bothered him that he owed me.

Anything you want Dave. Anything. I told him what I needed and he just nodded.

"No problem at all. I'll have to send to the big city...don't have such things around here. Have everything for you by six tonight, unless there is a real rush? "

I told him 6 pm would be fine. He finished his workout without further conversation. I read the paper.

On his way out, he came over to talk.

"Was thinking while I was working out. That ass hole Nails was in, looking for you a couple of days ago. Was asking that little gay guy that works out here usually in the mornings with the body odour guy where you were. Little guy has spunk. Said he did not know. Nails asked him where you lived. Same answer. Asked for your phone number. Same answer. Could tell Nails wanted to take it further, but he saw me here. He does not mess with me. Don't know if it has anything to do with your requests, but thought you should know either way. I'll see you here at six Dave."

That was it for the regulars I knew. A half dozen members I knew to say hi to, wandered in and out. Saturday mornings were always slow.

Then a guy came in that screamed cop, even though he was in plain clothes. He flashed me a badge to confirm what I already knew, and asked me if knew where Jeffrey Dalton was. That was Damion's partner. Told him no, it was slow today. Asked me if I had his address and phone number. Told him no, I was not the owner. Just worked here a few hours a week. He stared at me, trying to tell if I was telling the truth, then thanked me and walked out.

I looked up Jeffery's phone number in our files, and phoned him. Figured he should be told that the cops were looking for him. Didn't know why they were, but figured he had a right to know. My loyalties were to him, not some plain clothed that came in giving no explanation.

The phone was picked up on the fourth ring, but I hardly recognized the voice.

"Jeffrey, is that you?" It sounded like he was crying.

"Yes, who is it?"

"It's Dave from the gym Jeffrey. Sorry to bother you, but there was a cop in here looking for you. He did not say what for. Asked for your number, but I said I did not know it. Figured you should know. Sure they will find you sooner or later, and wanted to give you a heads up"

"Dave. They killed him! Damion is dead!" The grief in his voice was hard to take.

"I'm so sorry, Jeffrey. Damion is dead? The cops killed him?"

"No. No. I am a mess. Sorry. I don't know who killed Damion. Someone did. There were some of those biker guys outside taunting us when we went in, but I don't know if it was them. It was horrible. I came out of a bar we had been in. We had had a bit of an argument." Jeffery's story was coming out between sobs. " Damion left a half hour or so before me. I went to look for him, and there he was, outside the club in the alley. His face was a horrible mess. All cut up. No one would recognize him. I knew it was him because I recognized his clothes and the small mole he has...had... on his neck. Looks like a heart. And his trousers were drenched in blood. It was horrible." More sobs, and a long pause. They had cut off.....cut off. They had cut off his parts David, and stuffed them down his...... " he broke into sobs again. But, I knew what he was trying to say. "I just ran off. I couldn't handle it....."

"I am so sorry Jeffrey. Do you need company? Do

you want me to come over?"

"No, no Dave. You are so kind. Damion really liked you. I mean, not like *that* you know. He really liked you. Said you were kind. Said you were his friend. I'll be alright."

He did not sound alright to me, but there was little I could do for him. "Jeffrey. You have to phone the police. Talk to them before they find you. They will find you, Jeffrey. Explain to them how it was between you two. Tell them why you ran off. Tell them you saw bikers outside on the way in and they were giving you a hard time. Obviously other people will have seen them. Better you tell them now Jeffrey. They should understand. You have to call them, Jeffrey.

"Yes I will Dave, I will. Thank you."

He hung up, poor bastard. My heart went out to him. I could just hope things worked out for him OK. Despite his looks, he was a gentle soul. I hoped the cops would not take too long to figure that out.

I hate phones with a passion. Much prefer face to face conversations. Cannot understand for the life of me the world's preoccupation with smart phones. These days you even see people out on dates each talking to someone else on their phones. Seems weird to me.... but then again, I must seem weird to them...and there are a lot more of them that love phones than there are people like me that hate them.

But, today was my day for phones. I hung up from Jeffrey and phoned the number on the card I had given me a few days ago. The phone number for Nails.

The phone was answered on the third ring. A deep voice I would never forget said "Yea?"

"Nails. This is Paladin. I've been out of it the last few days. Johnny and I were in a pretty serious smash up a few days ago. Guess you know he's in hospital?"

There was no reply. I waited a few seconds and carried on.

"Thought about what you said. Sounds good. Real good. I would be stupid to pass it up. Realize that. Should have realized it then... but was worried about fall out. Been giving it a lot of thought. Indeed. Left the party early so I could think. I had decided it was the right thing to do the next morning. Bullwhip and I were on our way over to see you when we got fucked up. But, now something else has come up."

There was more silence on the phone. I just paused a second or two, and then continued.

"Got back into the gym I work at part time for the first time today.... been too banged up to work. Don't know if you know the gym, but Bullwhip has a lot of connections there. "
Another short pause by me, another interpretation of

"The Sounds of Silence" from the other end. This guy was a real pleasure to carry a conversation on with. I did not know if he was trying to intimidate me with the silences, or was just a man of few words. Actually, I did not give a shit. The conversation was going as I had planned.

"Guy that knows Bullwhip and knows we are tight dropped in to see me. Said he had a huge shipment of smack he wanted to move. Said the strength was not that hot, but the price was right. Said he had to move it...fast. He gave me some samples.... but I don't touch smack. I can't ask Bullwhip. He's out of the picture for a while. I figured you might know someone into smack. Someone we can unload it onto fast and make a quick buck. The guy is desperate to move it fast."

Finally, the man spoke. I had his interest. He said he was sure he could find someone to test it for us, and was sure he could move it. I was pretty sure I knew who the someone was that could test it out.

"Look Nails. Gambling is one thing. Heisting a game is no problem. The players aint gonna run to the cops. I figured that out. But. Heroin is a whole other ball of wax. I don't want no part of moving that. I trust you. That's it. I don't want to be involved any further than meeting you. I don't want anything for it. Heroin scares me. How be I meet you at the club house tomorrow morning with the samples. Just you and me. You let me know if the stuff is worth bothering with. If it is, I'll put you in touch with the guy. I know he wants it gone like yesterday, so I'll set up a meeting between you and him fast once you give me the say so. I trust you. "

I could hear his brain ticking over in the silence. I could think of several ways Nails could use this to his advantage.... I was betting he was mulling over at least ten times more ways than me, and selecting the best for him.

"Good man, Paladin. Yea,come up tomorrow around 8 am. I'll make sure we are all alone. I live here. Most of my guys don't get up until around noon, especially on a Sunday, but I'll tell them I want some privacy, just to be sure. This will work out good. I'll make sure you are looked after my man."

"Great Nails. Nine am tomorrow. Just you and me. See you then. "

"Just you and me. Guaranteed. Lets make some bread buddy."

Gee, now I was his buddy. Kind of made me feel warm all over.

One last phone call. I phoned the owner of the gym. Told him I would look after the gym for him today until 6 pm. Made him a happy man. He was a nice enough guy, and had a wife and kids he did not get to see often enough. I had just given him an unexpected vacation. I got all the papers I could, and sat down to read. Didn't feel like going home anyway.

Always amazed me that so little of any real importance made the paper. Way I saw it the world was going to hell in a hand basket with all the problems stemming from global warming and political corruption, but it was usually inconsequential drivel that made the stories, and when they did latch onto something a little out of the mundane, they beat it to death until it was just as boring as the rest.

Vito showed up as promised. A little early actually. Had a big smile on his face.

"Got everything you wanted Dave. It's all in here." He hoisted up one of the nicest gym bags I had ever seen. " The gym bag is a bonus. My gift to you. The other stuff is just the way you wanted it. I don't want to know your business Dave. But, I wish you well! Just be careful. Have a sneaking suspicion that what you are doing will actually put me more in my debt! Think it will make my life a lot happier. But, what do I know. Do what you want with this stuff. Catch ya later!"

Anyone else saying that would have made me very nervous indeed. I don't want people knowing my business. But, if there was one thing I was sure of, it was that Vito would never cause me any grief. I went home with the new gym bag, attached my carrier bags to my bike ready for the morning and went in for an early night. Usually, Saturday night was a night to party, but I had an important day ahead of me. If I survived tomorrow, I could party later.

CHAPTER 11

Ah, drugs, and the war on same. The war on drugs has been around a long time. The drugs are winning. Really, you should not be surprised. Good business for a lot of 'important people' who would hate to lose it. As a former US chief of police, Joe McNamara wrote in the National Review:

"It's the money, stupid. After 33 years as a police officer in three of the country's largest cities, that is my message to the righteous politicians who obstinately proclaim that a war on drugs will lead to a drug-free America. About $500 of heroin or cocaine in a source country will bring in as much as $100,000 on the streets of an American city. All the cops, armies, prisons and executions in the world cannot impede a market with that kind of tax-free profit-margin. It is the illegality that permits the obscene mark-up, enriching drug-traffickers, distributors, dealers, crooked cops, lawyers, judges, politicians, bankers, businessmen..."

It seems it has always been thus. Bayer had a trade mark on the name heroine way back in the 19th century, promoting it as 'the sedative for coughs." Handed out free samples through doctors. But by 1913, there were too many problem users, Bayer realized that the light at the end of the tunnel was a train rushing towards them, and backed off .They began pushing their other big seller, aspirin. In 1924 use of heroin was made illegal and from then on draconian law enforcement ruined far far more lives than the drug ever did. Bayer of course suffered no repercussions whatsoever.

Now, you could say that was not why they conveniently stopped selling heroine. You could say Bayer did not know the problems. You could say that. But, this is the same company that was part of I G Farben during WW2, the company that financed Josef Mengele at Auschwitz, the company that produced the poison gas that killed millions. Hell, they even had their own private concentration camp so that a ready supply of experiment subjects were close at hand. You think and say what you like, but I am a betting man, and I think and say you are wrong. Bayer came out of that smelling like a rose too. I tend to think Big Pharma is a hell of a bigger threat to the world than the drug addicted targeted. But, damn, they just about rule the world, so not much gets done to them.

That said, Heroin is a very addictive drug. Most of the stuff on the streets is watered down. Deaths occur from badly watered down product, or overdoses from product that is too strong. Once again, it is the illegality that causes this.

I had told Nails that I was bringing him samples of watered down, weak product. I lied.

I stuffed my nice new gym bag in the carrier, stuffed a few packages in my jacket pocket and went off for the meeting.

When I got there a little before 8, there were two big Harleys parked outside. I parked my Hardly beside them. Nails came to the door, wrapped his huge arm around me and led me in. Sitting there was another guy. Half Nails' size, but just as ugly.

He never even bothered to mention the deep bruises on my face. Awww. Here I thought he was my buddy, and he forgot to make nice. Got right down to it. "This is my vice president, Scraggs. I know I said we would meet alone, but you can trust Scraggs. He's going to help me judge the purity of the smack. You got it with you?"

The introduction struck me as funny, but I did not laugh. Here he was telling me I could trust Scraggs the day after he said I could trust him when he said we would meet alone. Maybe he just had trouble understanding the meaning of the word trust. Could be that. I also found myself wondering why the vice president was not held in higher esteem than the president in an organization that made its living off vice. My mind works like that. Scraggs presence was a problem, but not unexpected. I figured I could handle it. I just nodded to let him know I had the goodies.

There was a remote chance that Nails had brought Scraggs along to have him shoot up instead of himself, just in case I was bringing them drain cleaner, but I doubted it. I think Nails was convinced that no one in their right mind would even dream of pulling something over on him. Besides, psychopaths hate to be denied the instant pleasures of gratification. I breathed a sigh of relief when I saw that the draw of the needle was too much to overcome and he shot up first, then handed over to Scraggs. Both took really big hits because I had said the stuff was low grade. Nails took four times as much, I guess because he figured he was twice as big, and twice as important. He was the president.

Injecting heroin gives a fantastic high within seconds. Pupils of people that smoke grass become huge. With heroin they become tiny. Both these boys had pin pricks for pupils within seconds, and were grinning at each other like idiots. Nails turned to me slowly, and grinned at me.

"Sure you don't want some Paladin? You don't know what your missing."

I grinned right back. "No thanks, I'll pass. Sit back, relax. Enjoy. Then give me your opinion on whether I did good. "

He did just that. A few minutes later, he turned to me again. "You know, Paladin, you..........." There was a pause of about 15 seconds, and then he started up again as if he had not paused. "...said this stuff was low grade. I gotta........... another long pause...........tell you, this shit is good......"

I could not believe it. He was 'on the nod ' already. Heroin causes users to go on what is called 'the nod' especially if they have taken high doses. They don't even realize they are doing it, and can continue conversations as if they had never nodded off at all. Nails was nodding off deep. Scraggs was doing the same, but not to the same degree. I got up, shook him, and told him to come help me bring the rest in. Followed right along like an obedient puppy. But, whereas I would never kick a dog, when I figured we got far enough away from Nails, I kicked him so hard in the nuts I hurt my toes, even through my cowboy boots. Old habits die hard. I went to 'put the nut in' , but drew back at the last second: my head was still tender from my face plant on the pavement. However, I had brought a couple of rolls of quarters, and had them inside my fists. I gave him six hard belts below the belt. He folded with hardly a sound. Just a few gurgles. He puked all over the floor. Vito had told me that just one fill up on this stuff would kill the normal man.... but I was not taking any chances. I gave him two more. Then I went back to Nails, and gave him four more. After all, he was president and deserved more. He actually looked up at me as I was administering the first one, and smiled a dreamy smile. I told him to enjoy, and he closed his eyes. I would have preferred that he did not die happy, but, dead is dead. I dragged Scraggs back and sprawled him on the floor beside Nails. Gave them each one more needle each, just to be sure, then wiped off the needles, pressed them into their hands to get fingerprints, and tossed them around the floor. I cleaned up the worst of the puke and tossed the dirty rags in the toilet. Figured the little puke I left on the floor would never be noticed in that place. Had not been cleaned in years. Picked up my quarters. Waste not want not.

I went out to my carrier bag and got the gym bag. Took it inside. The bag had a half dozen hand guns in it. I had told Vito that I wanted wiped guns that could not be traced back to him, but that I had no problem with if they had been used in serious crimes. He understood.

Now came the hardest part of the whole thing: entering that incredibly filthy, disgusting toilet. I wanted to hide most of the guns in there. Had to hold my breathe, and leave my rubber gloves on.

I was out of the club house before 8:30. Only sounds were the birds.

I got home and took a nice long shower. Took the gym bag in there with me for a quick wipe, just to be sure. Then, I went out for breakfast. Couldn't go to Franks. Much too close to the club house. The place I found was not half as good, but I was hungry, and it was good enough.

CHAPTER 12

Went to the hospital after breakfast. The nurses told me that Johnny was out of danger, but still in very serious condition. I asked if I could talk to him, and they said yes, but only for a few minutes. That was all I wanted anyway.

I got the shock of my life when I walked into Johnny's room. It wasn't the looks of Johnny. His head was bandaged, and his eyes were closed. What bothered me was the feeling. That same icy feeling I got when ever I was around a psychopath was as strong as it had ever been with any of them...and I had never had that feeling around him before. I hesitate to say it, in case some bright spark in the military gets the idea that a ready supply of psychos could be useful to them and starts doing experiments, but I am fairly certain that if they experimented, a hefty diet of steroids, followed by a hit of LSD and a sharp metal object to the right part of the brain would do it for them. Might take years to find just the right mix, but I would not put it past them.

I tapped Johnny on the shoulder, and his eyes opened. The look he gave me was not friendly.

"Just dropped in to tell you Johnnie. I'm gonna pass

on Nails' offer."

"Your a stupid fuck Paladin"

"You could be right Johnnie. I think I've had enough
of city life. Time to leave. You look after yourself."
With that I got up and left. Stopped at the door to
look back, and a look of hatred was in his eyes. I did
not think I would miss Johnnie. Hoped I never saw
him again. Turned out, that was wish-full thinking.

I made a stop in the lobby of the hospital to make a
call to the police from the pay phone. I disguised my
voice with a cloth, and spoke quickly.

" Thought you guys should know. I was out at the
club house of the Evil Ones last night and a bunch
of them were laughing about a gay guy they had
beaten up and killed. Said they stuffed his balls in
his mouth. Don't like fags, but that ain't right if it's
true, so I wanted you to know. Also, saw them hide
hand guns in their washroom. Don't know if those
guns had anything to do with it, but thought you
should know. I aint going back there. Those guys are
bad news." I hung up before they could ask me the
usual 'who's calling' and 'where are you' type
questions. Like I was going to mention things like
that anyway. I figured they would go out and at least
check, and with a little luck a few of the gang would
have found the bodies and would be trying to figure
a way to hide them. Figured my crime scene would
be more than a little compromised by the time the
cops got there, and with a little luck, any suspicions

they had about Jeffrey would be forgotten in a flash once the cops got a hint of the Evil Ones as suspects. Cops like easy answers.

I went out and partied that night. Had a damn good time. Cant say I slept that well though when I returned. Me and a lady friend were too busy to sleep much.

Monday I got up, phoned the gym owner and told him I would not be able to fill in for him anymore, went to the bank, drew out cash. I had a horrible feeling that I was not done with The Evil Ones, and I have learned to always trust my feelings. But, for now I would put those feelings behind me. I was heading out on vacation.

CHAPTER 13

(This chapter deals a lot with poker. If you do not understand the basics of the game, you might want to check out the info starting on page 249. Or you can just 'bluff' your way through)
:-)

OK. Wasn't going to be a real vacation. More like a working holiday. I was going to do something stupid: I was risking everything I had on a trip to Nevada. If I made it big, I would be set for life. If I lost it all, I would have to start over again somewhere else. I bought a return ticket, just in case I really hit rock bottom, and tucked $200 in my boot so I would not be completely destitute. Sometimes in life, you have to take chances, and I was betting it all on a two week poker blitz. I can imagine a number of you tut tutting. Gambling for a living! What else? Gotta tell you, personally I think making a living off the sweat of some poor bastard making a dollar a day and selling these goods so cheaply that small businesses can't even come close to competing, manufacturing cars that are inefficient in their fuel use and refusing to try to improve the efficiency or the durability because it would not make as much profit , and/or manufacturing inferior goods that land up in land fill and help destroy the very planet we rely on all seem like worse ways to make a buck, and yet such people are revered. Guess I am missing something important. But I wont lose any sleep over it.

Casinos do not make nearly as much on poker as

they do on other games. By far the majority of people coming to gamble just want the rush of winning. It's really bizarre to watch someone getting all excited winning $15 on a slot pay off, ignoring the $200 he lost to get it. But, people love all those bells and whistles. And casinos love people playing slots. That is why there are so many of them ...the take is so much in the casinos favour it's criminal. But then, Vegas is run by the mob, so what can you expect. Next are the games like craps, roulette, etc. The take on each and every hand virtually guarantees that everyone will leave with nothing but memories of how they almost made it. Just as with the gym business, the very few that do make a few bucks are good for business, leading the rest of the sheep to the slaughter. Even when someone leaves a big winner, the casinos do not mind that much. They know that most of the big winners will come back and lose what they won, and then some. You do not have to worry about being cheated in a big Vegas casino .... almost everybody loses without them running fixed games, and that is just the way they like it.

Poker is a big draw these days, so they have to offer it. But, players are playing against each other. The casino makes money by taking what is called the rake. That can kill you on the smaller stakes games. You can live with it at the high end.

I settled in early Tuesday morning to play poker. Spent a rather frustrating day trying to find games big enough to make playing worthwhile. Soon found myself at the Bellagio. Back then, most of the big names in poker played at the Bellagio. The main poker room has 40 poker tables, and I was doing great at the highest limit games they had. I let it be known I was interested in getting into a game with a $50,000 buy in. That was about half of what I had by then, but I was not interested in grinding out a few thousand at a time: I had two weeks to make it or go bust. By Thursday afternoon I was in what is known as Bobby's Room. It is a small room off the main poker room, and I was in with the big boys. Some of the big names were there, and they were more than happy to have a few new faces join them. That is how they made their money. Playing just amongst themselves, they would all lose money, as the rake becomes the big winner against evenly matched opponents..... but new blood meant money in their pockets. Usually.

At the table I sat down at ,I completed the table. Nine players in total. Three guys I figured were pros. Two of them I actually recognized. One just acted like one. The other guys were probably all very wealthy individuals that did well in their local games and wanted to play with the best when they came to Vegas. Some of them were trying to look really tough. In most endeavours if your good, you don't have to try to impress; in poker, trying to impress is a tell. The game had a minimum $10,000 buy in, no limit to the amount you could bring to the table. True to my word, I dropped down $50,000. One guy bought in for $25,000, another was in for the same as me. The three pros bought in for

$100,000 each. I would have liked to have matched them, but I did not want to drop everything I had in my first big game. One other guy initially bought in for $50,000, then changed his mind to $100,000 when he saw the pros buying that. The other two bought in for $250,000 each! You never, ever, let them see you sweat, but inside I was beginning to wonder if that car accident had scrambled my brain. I had never in my life seen so much money riding on a game. Sure, it was only brightly coloured disks, poker chips, that were stacked up on the table. They are used on purpose, to lure you into forgetting that you are playing for money. Those coloured disks represented a ton of money!

The game went on and on, and I was winning more than I was losing. That was the important thing. Then I was dealt five jack suited. I was in the big blind position, meaning I had to put in two hundred dollars whether I wanted to or not, and wait to see what everyone else did. We were playing $100/200 no limit, which means the person in what is called the small bind has to bet $100, and the big blind, me, had to bet $200. There were 9 people at the table. Three of the people called my $200. Then it came to one of the pros. His first name is Daniel. He raised to $400. The other pro still left in the game , Phil saw that $400. The guy in the small blind position, who was already on the hook for $100, decided to drop down another $300 and stay in for the flop. I hesitated for a second or so. Five jack is pretty lousy hand, but I was already in for $200 and it was worth another $200 to see the flop. I reckoned the others that had called would either fold or call the raise.... it takes either a really smart player aiming to sucker people in by holding back initially on a big hand, or a real idiot to re raise against a couple of pros before the flop if they did not raise themselves when it was their chance. These guys were neither really smart or really stupid.... they were basic players.

One of the guys that had called my $200 was one of the guys that had bought in for $250,000 and he had been losing steady. I could tell he was really getting frustrated, but I did not think he was that dumb. He wasn't. Everyone stayed in, by calling the $400 bet, not raising. I was being given a chance at a $2,800 pot for just that additional $200 on top of the required $200 I had to put in anyway. I would have been crazy not to take that chance.

In No limit Hold'em, each player is dealt two cards that no one else can see. This is when the initial betting occurs, and where we were at this stage. Once the initial betting has occurred, five cards are laid on the felt face up, so that everyone can see them. But, they are not put down all at once. First, three cards are exposed. These three cards are known as the flop. Don't ask me why... they just are. You now have a pretty good idea of your odds of winning..... and if they aint good, now is the time to fold! A lot of people just can't seem to do that.

Remember those lines in Kenny Rodgers song, 'The Gambler' : " You've got to know when to hold 'em, know when to fold 'em, know when to walk away, know when to run" ?

90% of the time, the flop is THAT time. A lot of people lose a lot of money because they don't understand that.

Once the flop cards are on the felt, and viewed by all, more betting occurs.

Everyone gets to use the two cards in their hand, and three of the 'community' cards. You are betting that you can end up with the best hand at the end. It is all based on odds. The next card exposed is called the turn. Again, I don't know why. The final card is called the river. It is said that the name 'river' comes from the days of riverboat gamblers. Crooked players tried to substitute a card for the last one that would win them the pot. If they got caught, they ended up in the river!

The flop, the first three cards down on the table, came down as a jack and a pair of fives. The $250,000 buy in guy bet $10,000.

By now the smart people at the table knew his bets did not necessarily mean anything. Way too aggressive, he tried to drive out others way too often, thinking he could bully them with his larger stack. That was why he was losing steadily. Both Phil and Daniel called, as did I and one other player. The others folded. I did not know what they had, but I had a full house! 55JJJ. I could have raised, even gone all in, but that would scare people off. I reckoned I would leave the betting to the aggressive guy to my right. My heart skipped a beat when the turn, the fourth card to hit the felt, was another five! My full house had just improved to four of a kind! 5555.

A large part of poker is reading the other players' expressions and mannerisms. Little signals they give off when they have a good or a bad hand are called 'tells'. I had used a fake tell a couple of times in the game, letting a small sigh out just before I folded a hand. I'd done it for just this purpose, to be used for just a moment like this,when I had a monster hand and I wanted them to think they had me. I let the smallest of sighs escape my lips now. No one could see or hear my heart skip a beat, but I was hoping they would notice the sigh. I didn't know if $250,000 guy had noticed. I was damn sure Daniel and Phil did. $250,000 guy raised another $20,000. The two pros stayed in, the other guy folded. I paused long enough to make them think, then called, hoping they would think I had little, but was loathe to see such a big pot go without a fight. There was now over $130,000 in the pot.

Ah. What a thing when luck comes calling. The final card, the river, was an ace! The card most people online wait for. I figured $250,000 guy played a lot online, and that was the card he was waiting for. I knew he did not have another 5, 'cause I had it. I was fairly certain he did not have another jack: pretty sure one or both of them were with the pros. Damn sure he did not have three aces. Guys like that don't slow bet when they have ace ace in their hand, and if by some miracle he had, he would have re-raised after the pros were in with a raise. At best he had ace something, and was looking at the three fives and reckoning he had high hand,full house, two aces, three fives. He went all in with the remaining 90,000 from his original stake. Daniel folded. Phil matched him. I did not have enough to match them.... I only had 44,000 left in front of me. In that went. In no limit hold'em, "all in" means you bet everything you have, up to what the biggest amount in the pot is. You don't have to dig into your pocket and throw more on the table. DAMN. If I could have, I would....but that is not allowed.

Sure enough, $250,000 guy showed ace four, giving him a full house, ace, ace, five five five. He broke into a huge grin as he dropped them on the table. Phil showed no emotion when he put down ace ace, giving him a full house ace ace ace, five five. In hold'em, you use the best five cards out of the seven..... two in your hand, five communal cards on the table. A full house with three aces beats a full house with three fives. $250,000 guy had managed to lose his whole stack. He was almost in tears, and did not notice when I put down my jack five..... but Phil jolted back from what he thought was a sure thing. My four of a kind took almost $260,000 from the pot. Phil got what was left. $250,000 guy was now $0 guy. Phil looked at me and nodded, as if to say nice one. Daniel smiled at me.

The game kept going for another 9 hours. Phil dropped out about even with his original stake. Not his night. People dropped in and out of the game all that time. Most of them left a fair chunk of their stake with us. In the end, it was just Daniel and I.

By then he and I had been talking a fair bit. He was Canadian too, although he spent most of his time in the states. He was going to a big game as was Phil. At the Commerce Casino in Los Angeles. Sorry Dave, it's been a real pleasure playing with you, and getting to know you. But, I have a big weekend ahead of me. If I stay, you and I will just be battling it out, paying the casino. Would rather rest up. Tell you what though. If you feel like playing this weekend, I can get you an invite. You have to bring a minimum of $250,000 to the table, but I don't think that will be a problem for you" He looked at the stacks of chips in front of me and smiled. Think you'll have fun. Lots of faces you will probably recognize....but not from poker. Lot of the big stars in Hollywood love to gamble. I'd like to see you try your luck, and I know Phil. He will be dying to have another crack at you!" He smiled again.

What could I say. I was up to a little over $500,000! I should have said no, and gone home. A smart man would quit. But damn, I was not even into my second week, and even if I lost my $250,000 at the Commerce, I would still be further ahead than I had ever dreamed. Besides, no one had ever called me smart and got away with it....... I had come to play poker, and this was a dream come true.

I told Daniel that I would love to take him up on the offer, and if he was serious I would leave right now so that I could get used to the Commerce, as I had never been there. He smiled again. "David, I'll phone right now so that I don't forget. When you get there, book into the Crowne Suite Hotel. It's right beside the Casino."

CHAPTER 14

Most people think of Vegas when they think of poker. Truth is the largest poker casino in the USA is the Commerce. It boasts over 200 tables, non stop poker action...and no slots!!! 10,000 people a day play there, on average. You don't get the same number of totally clueless players as you can get in Vegas, but you do get a lot of incredibly wealthy patrons, including a large number of movie stars. Stars like to remain incognito if they can, so the casino does their best to accommodate them. The game I was going to was one of those games.

When I got to the Commerce, I checked in with the casino services, and was told I would be expected at the game starting at 5pm Saturday in their high stakes room. Daniel had been true to his word. They called me Mr. Dee athe, but I let it slide. I went to the Crowne, checked in and asked for a wake up call at 8pm. Action is always best in the evenings, and a man has to sleep. When I got up, I worked out in their gym, then went for a fantastic meal. For once in my life, I felt that expense was no object. Believe it or not, I could not live that life on a regular basis. It is just not me. But, I was on vacation, and I was waaay up. I watched for an hour or so, to get the feel of the place and the tables, then sat down to play another 100/200 no limit game. I played for about 4 hours, made about $20,000, and packed it in. There were some beautiful ladies walking around, but I wanted to be well rested, so I went back to my room alone.

Got up feeling great. Went for a workout, followed by a swim, then headed over to the casino for another great meal. I had been what they call comped: meals were free. Whatever I wanted.

When I got to the high stakes room, I paid my $250,000 and was directed to my table. There were 2 tables set up for the event, each person putting up $250,000. I smiled inwardly. Welcome to the big time Dave! I was not surprised to find that both Phil and Daniel were at my table. I figured Phil wanted a chance to get his money back. Still, there were no bad feeling. Losing was all part of the game.... a part I was hoping to avoid right now. I recognized two other people at the table. One was a famous tough guy from the movies, the other was a femme fatale. I will not use her real name. I'll call her Eve. Blond, beautiful, and enough to tempt any man without needing an apple. Tough Guy was a nice enough person in real life. Little full of himself, but who could blame him. He made tens of millions of dollars per movie, and was in high demand. He wanted to keep his gambling a secret, so I see no reason to mention his name. Tough Guy will do. I noticed.... who could miss... that Eve was just about falling out of her dress. I made certain to get an eyeful now, because when the game started, she could have stripped off naked and I would hardly notice. A lot of women in poker use their bodies as an advantage. If you want to win, you learn to tune it out. Phil and Daniel were both obviously well known to those at the table. I made it known that this was my first time ever playing at the Commerce, and the first time ever I had played in such a big game. I tried to sound nervous. Hey, in poker, you use any edge you can.

The first six hours were fairly uneventful. The tough guy and Eve had both lost everything and were working on their second buy in for $250,000 Did not seem to faze them in the slightest. Two of the others were down to about half . I was up to about $500,000, both Phil and Daniel had a little more than me.

So far, luck had been with me. I was praying that it would stay with me just a little longer. You cannot rely on luck. Well, that is not entirely true. The only sure thing you can rely on with luck is that it will change...and you never know when. You rely on your skill. But, when luck combines with skill, you can really get ahead. Anyone that tells you luck has nothing to do with winning at poker is a fool. Luck has everything to do with it. That is why it is called gambling. Luck has everything to do with everything to some degree. True, the harder you work, the more luck you will have, but if you have succeeded at anything in life and don't think luck had anything to do with it, you are just kidding yourself. You just never know when it will change. I was about to have to take a gamble on that.

Then,again I found myself sitting in the big blind in a similar situation to Vegas. This time everybody stayed in, and the two pros raised to $400. Once again I was sitting with a mediocre hand, nine and queen of spades, but once again there was too much money in the pot to fold without seeing the flop. As Yogi Berra is famous for saying, "It's like deja vu all over again." I was already in for $200, so called and dropped in another $200. Everyone followed suit. The flop came down as ten jack of spades and the ace of diamonds. There was a raise of $10,000 and everyone stayed in! I looked over at Phil. He smiled. It is very rare to see any emotion showed at a poker table, but I knew he was not giving anything away. Like me he was thinking back to our last game together, and could see the similarities. I was hoping he was thinking lightning cannot strike twice. I was praying it would. Then came the turn, and another ace hit the felt , the ace of spades, Tough Guy went all in for another $200,000. Phil went all in also...for the tune of over $500,000. A little more than I had. I could be pretty certain Phil had four aces,or possibly a full house once again with three aces, but this time with two jacks. Once again, he looked at me and smiled. He wanted Tough Guy all to himself.

I knew all eyes were on me. I reckoned that if I was going to contemplate throwing in around a half a million,I was entitled to a minute to think about it. I think Phil was pretty sure I was just playing hard to get, waiting to fold so that he would not think he could intimidate me. But no, I was thinking of going all in. I had nine ten jack queen ace of the same suit.

An ace high flush. I was pretty sure that was what Tough Guy had. If he had the king, he beat me. Otherwise, I beat him. But, that didn't really matter. I could be pretty certain Phil had a hand that beat us both. Normally I would have folded without a moment's hesitation. But I had a really strong, almost overpowering feeling that I would regret folding for the rest of my life.

Remember I told you about my grandfather's feeling, and how it saved his life? And, how I figured my feeling around psychopaths was related? I believe all people started off getting such strong feelings. Civilization has made it so that 99.9% of all people suppress such feelings, ignore them totally. Of the other .1% , 99% rely on those feelings way too much, and think they feel them way more often that they do. I reckoned I fell into that 1% left over. I knew the feeling I got around psychos had never let me down, and I believed my grandfather's story. I knew most people did not. I had never, ever allowed a 'feeling' to influence my poker. But, damn this feeling was strong!!

To put things in perspective, the odds of getting a flush are about 500to1. A full house? About 700 to 1 Four of a kind? About 4,000 to 1. Then things start getting hairy. Odds of hitting a straight flush? About 70,000 to 1. Odds of hitting a royal flush, which is a straight flush from ten to ace of the same suit? About 650,000 to 1! I'd played a lot of poker, and had had straight flushes a few times. I had never had a royal flush. But, I kept thinking. If I called and lost, I was still way ahead of where I came in. If I folded and the right card showed up, I would never forgive myself. I would feel stupid ....but I would never see any of these people again, so why should I care if I looked and felt foolish?

My revelries were interrupted by the dealer saying "I am sorry sir. You must either call or fold."

I was in the state of California, the state of Harry Callahan of Dirty Harry fame. I thought of his line: "you've gotta ask yourself one question: 'Do I feel lucky?' Well, do ya, punk? " I did. I looked at Phil. I shrugged. I went all in.

Sure enough, Tough Guy had the king, the highest flush possible , and Phil had four aces. With the king in Tough Guys hand, the royal flush still eluded me. The river was an eight of spades, giving me 8 to queen of the same suit. I had a straight flush! Gasps came from around the table, except from Phil. For once his cool was broken. "Fuck! Not again!" he instantly regained his composure, and apologized to Eve, but I don't think she had even noticed. Then he stood up and shook my hand. I had just made well over $1,000,000 on one hand!

"Sorry Phil. That was a bad beat. I just had the strongest feeling that I had to stay in. Never had that before. Too strong to ignore."

He looked at me and smiled. " I know that feeling. Rare, but you have to go with it." It was then that I realized that Phil, and probably Daniel, were two more of that ever so tiny minority that relied on that feeling without overdoing it. That was what made them the poker pros that they were.

I stood up. "It has been a real pleasure. I mean that. It's not just the money.... although you can bet your ass it has a lot to do with it. I know just how fickle lady luck can be. I'm cashing in. I wish you all the best of luck. I have had more than my share tonight. Far more than my share these last few days. Time to quit."

I thought lady luck was finished with me, but I was wrong. Eve stood up and cashed out of the game with me. Asked me for a drink, her treat. I smiled, and said I figured I could afford to buy her one. As it turned out, the Commerce insisted all drinks were on the house, and neither of us had to pay. I took my sunglasses off and explained the black eyes. She just smiled and said we could leave the lights off if the way I looked bothered me. I left the waitress a hundred dollar tip...the first and last time I have ever done that.... and then we went to Eve's penthouse suite, and I got lucky in an entirely different way. Several times. The lights stayed on most of the night, and did not bother me a bit.

Next day, mid afternoon, I returned to my room and went to check out. The management insisted that the stay was on them. Indeed, if I wished to stay, they would move me up to a much nicer room. I told them I had to leave, but would be sure to stay with them if I returned. They assured me that next time all I had to do was ask, and everything was on them. Ah, how the rich and famous live. But, the truth was, I was never coming back if I could help it. I had more than I had ever dreamed possible just one week ago. Money had never been the be all and end all for me, but now that I had it, I knew exactly what I wanted to do with it. Living the life of a professional gambler had no part in that plan. This life was nice for a while, but I knew damn well it would destroy the 'me' I liked if I stayed. I knew exactly what I wanted to do, and intended doing it.

CHAPTER 15

When I got back to the Steeltown gym, everyone was pleased to see me, and ribbed me for still being pale after a week's vacation.

"Guess you got lucky and never left the room, eh Dave?" They did not know exactly where I had been and would never have believed the truth if I told them, so I just smiled. The owner wanted me to come back to work on the weekends, but I told him I was leaving town. Jeffrey told me the police had come to see him and were pursuing another line of enquires, but had no firm evidence. They seemed satisfied with his version of what had happened. He had tears in his eyes as he spoke to me. Could tell he was still pretty upset. Derek told me he had mentioned our last discussion to his father, who had taken the necessary precautions. He had also heard however that the guy who I mentioned was plotting the robbery had died of an overdose, so probably the worry was over. Better safe than sorry though. He thanked me again, and said that the location of the games I played in had been changed for safety reasons. Did I want him to inform everyone I was back? He knew they enjoyed our games together. I told him to pass. Fact was I was pretty well done with playing poker for money. Was going to take off on a driving tour of the countryside, and would not be around anymore. Indeed, had basically dropped in to say goodbye. He looked puzzled for a while, then broke into a big grin. When he smiled, his whole face lit up.

"Dave, you are a hard man to understand. But,whatever you do, I wish you well." He gave me his home number and address. No one else there would have expected it to be an address in the area of million dollar homes. I did. "Drop in if you are around, and keep in touch" I told him I would. Then we got down to a serious work out, spotting each other when required.

Vito came in when I was just about finished. He smiled, and moved his head ever so slightly; an invitation to come over where it was quiet,for a chat.

"Dave my man. Welcome back. I guess you heard that Nails and his buddy, Scraggs, died out at their clubhouse of overdoses?" I nodded. He smiled again. Terrible accident. Seems the cops went out there with warrants after an anonymous tip, just in time to find a bunch of the guys trying to bury them in the back yard!! They swore they found them OD'd in the club house and were just giving them a decent burial. Cops ordered the whole yard dug up! Then, the cops went inside and found all sorts of guns, many of them tied to crimes in the big city. Found tons of drugs too. Enough shit happening to keep those guys busy for years! Knowing the cops, I doubt they can make anything stick unless they play dirty...and I would not put that past 'em.... but being an Evil one will be a real disadvantage for some time. Hear a lot of the guys that were not at the clubhouse have split. Just the hard core element left." He grinned again. " Like I said earlier, reckon I owe you more now than I did before."

I just smiled. Told him I was going on an extended driving tour, and was not sure if I would ever be back. He was genuinely sorry to hear I was going, but, like Derek wished me the very best. Like Derek, he gave me his home number, and told me to call anytime. He also told me that he would spread word around Little Italy. If he was unavailable, he would let everyone know that whatever David Death wanted,was to be given him without question. I knew if I was ever in a tight spot, he would come through for me.

I went home, packed my clothes in my bike carriers, gave everything that did not belong to the landlord to my neighbour, and hit the road. I could have bought a Harley if I wanted, but my Hardly suited me just fine.

CHAPTER 16

Driving around was fun. I worked out in any gym I came across, paying the day fee if requested, but most of them let me work out one day for free. I ate in roadside diners mostly, and stayed in motels. Washed my sox and underwear in the motels, and when my other clothes got dirty, I stopped at a thrift store and bought second hand. Got to see a lot of thrift stores that way. Picked up books to read there too, along with the local papers that gave me a great incite into the places I was visiting. During my travels, I must have stopped in a hundred thrift stores. Always totally amazes me what people discard in our disposable society.

I enjoyed moving around for about four months . If I came across someone at one of the gyms, a waitress or hairdresser that was pretty, and showed an interest, I hung around for a few days. But, I always made it known up front that I was just passing through. Some of the married ladies that went to the gyms were absolutely incredible. There is an expression in the gym business : 'gym disease' That's when an owner or instructor in a gym falls for one of his married clients. Can lead to all sorts of headaches. Lot of the women I got to know matched Eve in beauty and physical fitness. Had several tell me that they were trophy wives who's husbands preferred to chase money than chase them. Seemed to me their husbands had their priorities all mixed up. I hope they got what they wanted out of life. I got what I wanted, and moved on. I was looking for a home, but having fun while I looked.

In the last month of my travels, twice I read about the mysterious disappearances of attractive young women from the towns I was visiting or had visited. Police could find no common link among the women, other than their attractive appearance. I was surprised I could still find women to go out with me, but I guess I don't have the looks of a guy to be afraid of, despite my size. But then when you think about it, guys like Bernardo don't look scary either. Bernardo. Now <u>there</u> was a psycho I would have loved to send on his way from this planet. The misery one man can cause.

My wandering came to an end when I fell in love. Wasn't gym disease. Indeed, there was not a gym in the town where it happened. It was in a town called Beaver Valley, and it was the town itself I fell in love with. I had travelled thousands of miles looking, only to find my idea of Eden equidistant from Steeltown and Hardrock. Could have driven there from either place in less than two hours. The travelling had been fun, but now it was time to settle down and put the plans I had been formulating into practice.

There were eight thousand people in Beaver Valley, a clean tidy town nicely laid out with small parks and tree lined streets, and surrounded by farm land and incredibly beautiful forests. There was a clear river running through the middle of town, no big big box stores or even chain stores, and friendly folks that seemed genuinely interested in getting to know you, and pleased to see you again once they had. This was not the phoney friendliness you get in cities when someone wants your business..... they were just nice. There were no big businesses, other than an ice cream manufacturer that made some of the best ice cream I had ever tasted, a cheese factory that made some of the best cheddar, a couple of factories making hand built furniture, and no less than two microbreweries who's beer was so good it sold to folks for hundreds of miles around, as they battled between each other always trying to make a better beer than the other. What a far cry from the big breweries who were always trying to make more profit that the others, but seemed to think of quality, as second to profits.

The rest of the stores were all privately owned small affairs. The restaurants were all owned by people that knew how to cook from scratch, rather than the chains that dominate every city, that knew how to make the optimum amount of money, but little else. That I always figured was why their food was always so lacking in taste, apart from the fats, sugars and salts they relied on to cover their deficiencies. I decided to stay for a few weeks to see if I was missing some flaw to what was to me a perfect hometown. Few weeks later, I decided to stay forever when I read in the local paper that the town council had rejected a proposal by one of the big box stores to build. They liked their town the way it was. So did I.

I looked around town in those two weeks, and found everything I needed. I found a nice little house that was an exception to the rule. An older couple had lived there until frailty had demanded a move to a nursing home. They fought that move to the bitter end, and the house had suffered. The yard was a mess the outside had needed a good coat of paint ten years ago, and the inside was no better. Couple of windows boarded up, wood floors stained and scratched. A real fixer upper. But there was no structural damage that I could see.

I phoned my parents and had told them I wanted to pick them up on the weekend and take them on a sort of mini vacation. They were curious, but I refused to tell them anything. Just told them to be ready. They had not been on any sort of a vacation since as far back as I could remember, so I knew they were excited. Mum told me they could never go anywhere without Scamp, their old mutt that I had grown up with. As if I did not know that. They had always had a dog, even when dad had trouble putting food on the table for us. A dog was part of the family. I told them Scamp was no problem...just bring his bed and food, and enough clothes for themselves for a couple of days.

Friday, I rented a car and drove over to pick up my mum and dad. Beaver Valley was just 100 miles from their town, a two hour drive at most. Only a hundred miles, but a whole new world. No grime or noise from the mines, no smell in the air, and clean water and green trees everywhere. On the way there I explained that I had made a lot of money...a LOT... playing poker, and was planning on settling down. No more living the life of a card shark. Luck like mine never lasted in cards, and I had given up making a living that way. I had done better than I had ever dreamed possible, and I was going to open a gym and put down roots. I explained that before the mini vacation started, I needed them to look at some places with me, to help me make decisions. They seemed pleased.

When we got to the house I took them inside. I had explained to the agent that I would probably be buying it, just wanted my parent's approval, and wanted to take them there alone. She had looked at me funny...a 230 lb grown man needing approval from mum and dad? But,she had let me have the keys, as I had already bought from her the day before, so she knew I was serious, and besides, the house was empty. I told mum and dad I was hoping they could help me fix it up.

Mum and dad looked around and I could see they were both pleased. Like me, they reckoned there was nothing that a little hard work could not fix up. There was a large outbuilding in the back of the house. The old guy that had lived there had run a repair shop out of it for years. I had been watching them talk amongst themselves, so when he spoke, I knew dad spoke for both of them. " The house is fantastic son. Nothing that we can't handle. But, we don't get vacations for another 4 months. Can you live with it like this until then? And, are you sure that building out back will be big enough for a gym? You know best, but I would have thought it was too small. And, what about zoning? Will they allow a gym here? "

That's when I told them. Told them I had already found and bought another building for the gym, an old feed store that had been sitting vacant on the edge of town for about a year. The store had moved to bigger and better things further out in the country, and no one had been able to find a use for the old place. Indeed, I had already got the blessing of the major for putting a gym in it. It did not hurt that the major had owned the feed store before I bought it.

I told them that what they said was enough for me, and I would buy the house we were looking at now. It was a great deal. But, I needed them to look at an old farm house a couple of miles outside of town I was thinking of buying as well. The land was just what I was looking for, and I reckoned the house could be fixed up fairly easily. It too had been sitting vacant for almost a year. Nothing too much wrong that I could see, but I wanted their judgement, and help to fix it up if possible.

They looked puzzled. "Dave. We only get two weeks off a year. Glad to help when we can, but two places in two weeks? We can come down weekends too, to get you going, but it will take a lot of time. If the price is right on this one, why not buy it and the feed store? Surely that's enough to keep you busy for a while?"

"Oh, the price is right dad. It's a steal. So is the one out in the country. The country one will be my dream come true. This one is for you and mum... your dream come true. I'll set you up with a repair and handyman business out of the building in back of here. If I'm going to start living the life I always wanted, I want you to as well. I really want to do this. It's about time I paid you back for being such great parents, and made up for being such a handful when I was a kid. Told you I did well. I can afford all three and the renovations."

I expected a lot of argument, and I got it, but I was adamant. Have always been a stubborn bastard. I told him I knew damn well he could make a good living in Beaver Valley doing renovations and repairs: was not much available in the town since the old guy that had lived here had packed it in. Explained I was going to need help with the building of the gym, and the repair of my home, so I would be his first customer. I'd supply him tools, Christmas presents for the next 20 years in advance. Would save me the hassle of having to look every year for gifts. They would live rent free in exchange for helping me, and could build up a profitable business from other people who would need their services. I would have gladly given them the house, but knew they would not take it. As it was, it was the first time I ever saw tears in my old man's eyes.....but they were tears of joy, so that was OK. They caved and agreed., and we went on to look at the other two places.

They agreed with my assessments. Same lady had all three listings and she was ecstatic when I paid cash for the two houses. I had already paid a healthy deposit on the old feed store. Think it was the best pay day she had that year.

Not too many people want to buy places in the country unless they are suitable for weekend retreats or within commuting distance to the job in the city. How they spend hours in the car each day driving to and fro is beyond me, but they do.

City folk buy weekend retreats, then they rush up from the city every second week or so. The husband spends his time riding around on a riding lawnmower, beer in hand, and the wife cleans the house of two weeks dust. Then they rush back to the city after their 'weekend vacation'. Most of them give up after a few years, and never do see the attraction. They sell their place to another hapless city couple. This place was not suitable for that type of couple: no lawn at all, except for a few yards around the house to keep the mice and other critters at bay, and a sorry site to look at inside. But, the basics were sound, and I figured it was repairable It had 25 acres that went with it. Mostly forest and wild grass clearings, but way too small for a farm even if all the land was cleared . A beautiful piece of land with it's own pond and a lot of potential for the retreat I wanted, but useless to most locals, and way too run down for city folk.

People that live in big cities would be absolutely amazed at what you can buy in rural areas for a song. I got all three places two owned outright and one with a manageable mortgage for less than I would have paid in full for a ticky tacky house in a city suburb which looked the same as all the other ones crammed together on postage stamp sized lots. In an incredibly beautiful setting and friendly neighbours. Granted, places in the country do not go up in value anywhere near as fast as those in the big cities. Not nearly as good an investment. But, I was not looking for an investment, I was looking for a home. I will never understand the city mentality. And they think country folk are dumb....

I could have paid the feed store off, and left no mortgage, but decided not to. If the gym could not support me and itself, then it was not worth running. This will truly sound crazy to most of you, but I had already told my accountant that at the end of the year, when I was finished setting up to my satisfaction, and after he had ensured that the government had received the taxes it required, I would be giving away the money I had to charities, all but a $20,000 buffer in the bank. As it was I would be far better off than most, and had no desire to hoard money. It was Gandhi that said "Live simply, so that others can simply live." Way better man than me. I had grown up poor and wanted to be comfortable. I would set myself and my family up nicely, then live simply after that. I wanted to be comfortable, but had no desire to be one of those people that are never satisfied, always wanted more. That is a sickness that creeps up on people if they are not careful.

I needed my dad to give me an idea of all the supplies he would need to fix up the three places. We went back to each place in turn, and he made me up detailed lists. Then I put them up in the same motel I was staying at where I had already made sure dogs were allowed, and told them to explore the town, their new home. I took them out to breakfast, lunch and supper at local restaurants. Restaurants were something they could never afford. When I drove them home Sunday they were both excited about the move that was to happen in two weeks. I had told them I would arrive with a truck and load them up. Told them to give the landlord their notice, and tell the guy he worked for as a minimum wage security guard to take his job and shove it. I knew mum would have no problem with notice at her job. I would be back in two weeks to pick them up and move them to their new home. They had always been the type to show me affection, but I had never had so many hugs and kisses. I knew damn well they had never had any real breaks in life. I was going to do my damnedest to change that.

CHAPTER 17

The next two weeks were busy as hell for me. People in big cities love their Big Box Stores. Me, I hate 'em. Some fat cat using slave labour in a far away land ,to make junk that he can sell cheap and drive small businessmen in his own country out of business while he gets even richer still? Junk that would end up in landfill. Big always wants more, and are never satisfied with what they have. I could not avoid all the junk, but I tried my damnedest, and I shopped locally in Beaver Valley for everything I could. I would much rather pay a few bucks more and keep a small businessman afloat. Actually,when you got right down to it, the amount you pay extra really is negligible.

I got up early and had breakfast next door to the motel. There had been another suspected abduction in a town about 20 miles from Beaver Valley. People in the coffee shop were all talking about it. People were getting worried. That was pretty close to home. Three in three months.

I went out to the local building supply, and hammered out a great deal for all the supplies I would need for all three places. I mentioned in advance, that on anything that it would be advantageous for him, I had no objection to cash.

Dad had not mentioned the need for new bathroom and kitchen fixtures and appliances, figuring the old ones still had a few years in them..... but I bought new fixtures for both places. Got jacuzzi style tubs for both places, big enough for two people. Knew damned well I would be using mine, and was pretty certain mum and dad had never seen anything like them. Arranged for someone to come out and measure for new kitchen sinks for both also, along with custom cupboards and granite top counters. Bought a complete set of tools for my dad, including a heavy duty belt sander for the floors. Arranged for Randy's wife to come out and select new lighting fixtures. Both places had solid maple floors in great basic shape, but sad looking from decades of neglect. Knew they would look spectacular once they were taken down to fresh wood. Then I bought all the supplies my dad had said we would need. Turned out that Randy, the owner of the Building Supply store could also get appliances. Bought new fridges, stoves, washers and dryers. I had learned to cook from my mum, and knew she did not like microwaves or dishwashers. Neither did I. But, made sure we had the best gas stoves available. Much easier to adjust gas elements.

I asked Randy if he knew where I could get furniture. Turned out he was best of friends with one of the guys that made furniture in town. He gave me an intro, and told me if I did not mind paying cash, the owner would sell to me at wholesale. I smiled. Cash was not a problem.

I had a little over seven and a half thousand feet of floor space to work with at the old feed store. Five thousand feet in the main room, which would be the main gym. Separate from the main gym, I had a room of about 700 square feet that would be for the heavy weight section. Another room of the same size would be for aerobics. The rest of the space would be change rooms, showers and washrooms. Not huge by city standards, but more than enough for a town of eight thousand people.

Gym equipment is like cars. Depreciates like hell as soon as it leaves the factory floor. People in cities always want to have the latest , the new and improved. If you knew what to look for, and where to look, you could get spectacular deals and top quality equipment from a gym that had gone belly up or was upgrading to the latest look. I knew where to look and what to look for. In fact, I knew that one of Vito's cousins was in the business of bankruptcy liquidation, and often cleaned out gyms in the big city. I often suspected that some of the merchandise he dealt in "fell off the back of trucks". Another of Vito's cousins owned a trucking company. Ah, the beauty of big Italian families. I phoned Vito, who was genuinely pleased to hear from me. I told him what I wanted, and he promised to call me back after he made a few calls.

When Vito called back, I had a deal for all the equipment I needed for far far less than what it would cost new. Vito promised to deliver it himself. We had a lot to catch up on. I told him I looked forward to it. Delivery within two weeks. I had forgotten to ask for the equipment to set the gym up with surveillance and 24 hour access without 24 hour staffing. Could he find it? He promised to call me back after he made a few calls. When he did, less than an hour later, the answer was the same as always: "Not a problem" Once again, deep discount. Vito was a very good man to know!

I bought myself a really nice computer at the local computer store, and had the owner set it up for me at the motel. Using a computer is easy, but setting the suckers up is beyond me. As soon as it was set up, I began surfing Kijiji . I found deals on two diesel crew cab pickups, one for me and one for my dad, and a large cargo trailer that dad would be able to use for his business. Both of the trucks had heavy duty hitch systems already hooked up, as is usually the case with trucks in the country. Mine also had a set up to pull a goose neck house trailer. Bonus! That was my next purchase: a really nice house trailer. I had really enjoyed travelling the past few months. I may have found the ideal home, but I still intended to take off when the urge hit me. Until then, I reckoned it would make a great home for me while I waited for the farm house to be redone. I could park it at the gym to be close while I renovated. Both of them were exceptionally hard workers. Mum had had heart problems from when she was a little girl, but she kept herself in shape, and knew how to pace herself . Dad to me had always seemed indefatigable. They would have their place fixed up in no time.

Next morning I got up bright and early, had breakfast, then headed over to see Randy at the building supply. I had felt a connection to Randy. Struck me as a really nice guy. Hard working, smart, honest and fair. He greeted me with a big grin, and invited me into his office when I said I needed a favour.

"Randy. I am setting my dad up here as a handyman. There is not too much he can't do, knowledge wise, but he only has one good leg. Left one is gone at the knee. Most time you cant tell, a little bit of limp is all. But some jobs, especially those involving ladders are a problem. I want to arrange an assistant for him. Someone not afraid of hard work, honest, with a driver's license. If he's all I asked for just now and he gets along with my dad, I can promise you my dad will look after him. They don't come any fairer than my dad."

"Think I have just the man for you. Local boy. Tom. 22 years old. Lost his left hand as a kid in a farming accident. Has trouble finding work because of it. Well, that and the fact that he was in and out of trouble in school. But, he's smart, and I've seen him work and know he can do better with one hand than most people with two. Really nice guy. Honest as the day is long. If the handicap and the lack of formal schooling don't bother you, sure he would work out great."

"Not going to bother me, and I am sure it wont bother my dad. If he can be depended on, that is what matters. Send him round to see me at the motel after supper will you?"

"Will do Dave. Like I said, his name is Tom. I'll have him drop around to the motel sevenish."

I had scouted all the residential streets, but decided to spend the rest of the day walking all around the commercial part of town, making myself familiar with it and the people that worked there. Started out at the east end, where my gym was going to be. I was more than a bit surprised to see a beautiful 74 cubic inch chopped Harley sitting outside the first building I came to, a building about half the size of the feed store, with a large high fenced in area at the back. The tiny sign by the door said "Sonny and Sue's" Nothing else. Certainly had my curiosity.

I walked in the door and was greeted by an old lab who came over to sniff me, tail wagging. There was a beautiful girl sitting at a potter's wheel. Jet black hair, sparkling blue eyes, delicate features. Born with natural good looks, it was her personality that shone through and made her beautiful...the kind of beauty that lasts for a lifetime. A tiny little thing, it seemed as if her smile was the biggest thing about her. Her hands were wet with slurry, so she wiped them on her apron and stuck out a hand. " Hi! I'm Sue. Excuse the mess. We don't get too many visitors.... but you are more than welcome! See you like dogs, and they like you. That's Cleo. You here to see Sonny, or just want to look around? "
Some people give off an aura of genuine goodness

and you feel as if they are really glad to see you. Sue was like that. Could tell I was going to like her. I introduced myself, and explained that I was brand new in town, had bought the old feed store, and I was opening up a gym. Explained I was just getting to know the town, and as they were my closest neighbours, I was starting with them. I apologized if I should not have come in, as they were obviously not a retail location. The door was open, and I had thought it was a store.

I would not have thought it possible, but her grin became even more luminous.

"Hell, no worries! I've lived here all my life, and Sonny has lived here since he was sixteen. We know everyone in town, and I just didn't recognize you. What I should have said is we don't get too many new faces in here. We wholesale mostly. But, we are always open to walk ins.

A gym! Oh wow. You picked the right place to start! You have no idea. You just got your first two customers! But, a gym! You've got to meet Sonny." She turned towards the back of the store, stuck two fingers in her mouth and let loose a piecing whistle. She turned back to me with an impish grin on her face "Sorry about that. Sonny's banging around in the back . About the only thing he hears is my whistle."

A cloth curtain parted and a man entered from the back into the front of the store. He actually had to turn slightly sideways to get through the standard size opening. I'm a big guy. Lots of muscles. This guy made me feel tiny! Sonny was naked to the waist. That waist was large in comparison to most people's....but tiny in comparison to the rest of him, and there was not an ounce of fat to be seen. The stomach muscles rippled as he turned to make it through the door. That stomach was thick with tremendous muscles from obviously heaving around huge weights. Besides, the incredible chest made the waist look tiny in comparison. The chest was covered in sweat. At the end of the most muscled arm I had ever seen was a fist that looked as if it could punch through brick walls without a problem. In the fist was a ten pound mallet, that he carried as if it was a tack hammer. He used the other hand to wipe long dark hair soaked in sweat from his eyes. His eyes flicked over quickly to see that Sue was OK, in case the call to attend had been a matter of urgency, then fixed his eyes on me. His grin matched Sue's :big white teeth in a tanned face. Thank god for that smile! I have never been one to cause innocent people trouble, but I could not help thinking how I would have reacted if I had come in to rob the joint or hassle Sue! No man had ever intimidated me before, not even Nails, although I knew he had tried hard to do so. Sonny did. Now I knew how other people felt when they first met me! I had always tried to put people at ease when first meeting them, because I often saw fear in their eyes for what I thought was no reason. I made a mental note to try harder. Sonny had obviously learned that lesson long ago. The smile was genuine and disarming. The huge hand that came out to shake mine had just the right amount of pressure. He had obviously judged my strength well. He did not want to insult me with less than a firm handshake, but he and I both knew he could have crushed it painfully.

"Sorry for the appearance. I make concrete items some days, do blacksmithing others. Today is a blacksmithing day.... been working over the forge. Damned hot. I'd do it totally naked but Sue wont let me."

"We can't have you toasting any important parts Sonny! This is Dave. He just moved here, and is opening a gym next door in the old feed store. He just dropped in to say hi and to look around. Told him we would be his first customers."

"Got that right. My work keeps me fit, and I have a few weights here to try and keep everything in proportion, but could use a proper gym. And Sue could use one. Sits at that wheel all day, getting fat." He looked at her and grinned. She stuck her out her tongue at him.

"Are you going to have aerobics Dave?"

"Hoping to. Have a room all planned out, but will need an instructor."

"Actually, I work out with Dawn from the bookstore, a long with a few other friends. Dawn is a really good instructor.....but we have to do the aerobics in her store, and there really isn't much room. You might be able to talk her into instructing .... tell her I told her to." She grinned again. One of the nicest grins I had ever seen. Her and Sonny were obviously very happy. Sonny was a lucky man.

"I will. I don't want to keep you guys from what you were doing. If you don't mind, I'll love to look around at what you do, then head on and see what else is in town. Can I just poke around, while you just get on with work?"

In unison, both of them said, "go for it". Sonny said "See you back here in a while. Cleo will keep you company." He turned slightly to fit through the door, and disappeared. Sue bent back to her wheel.

Her work was incredible. I had never seen such colours in clay, and her pots and bowls were delicate and graceful. Later I would find out she had developed her own technique for colouring porcelain clay by using various dyes and mixing them into the porcelain with what is known as a pug mill. She then put balls and slices of clay together in different colours, left them together under pressure, and after a few days, threw them on the wheel. The result was a line of unique pottery with a kaleidoscope of colours intermingled right into the clay, that I found out was in demand all over North America. I walked over to where she was working, waiting until she was finished the piece she was throwing.

"Sue, your work is beautiful" She rewarded me with one of her smiles. "I want to buy a couple. I want one for my mum. My mum and dad will be moving into town in a couple of weeks and want her to have one in her new home. Gotta have one for myself too. Right now, want to see what Sonny does, then I'm heading into town to explore. So far, I love my new hometown. OK if I drop in later to buy them? Don't want to carry them with me all day."

"If Sonny's bike is outside, we're here Dave. We work when we feel like it....but you'll usually find us here. We both love what we do. Sonny sometimes drives an old ambulance if he is going out with deliveries. His stuff is heavy, and the ambulance works great. When he's away, I drive a little 450 cc Honda." Sonny wanted to buy me a Harley, but can you imagine someone my size trying to control one of those?" I grinned my reply. "If there is a vehicle outside and if the door is open, drop in anytime!"

I walked through the curtain, painfully aware that I did not have to turn sideways...inches to spare. The sight that greeted me was almost surreal. Off at the back of the shop, Sonny was working on a huge metal sculpture of a tree. Large flames rose above him from the fire he was working on, his back to me. The muscles of his back rippled as he used the ten pound hammer to bend the glowing red iron to the shape he desired. If any of you saw the incredible hulk series on TV, the star,Lou Ferrigno, was 315 lbs, and 6 foot five inches tall. I was pretty sure Sonny had him beat by a long shot. I had never seen another man like it.

I wandered around the room. It was filled with sculptures in iron on one side of the room, along with sections of intricately worked iron fencing, and some farm implements he had obviously repaired. On the other side, were works in concrete, ranging from unique birdbaths and pedestals to smaller objects. As I got closer to where Sonny was working, I stopped dead in my tracks. There on a bench, were a half dozen sculptures that looked remarkably similar to the things I had seen on the top of my door that morning soon after the crash. Nothing could ever capture the pure evil that the 'originals' had exuded, but the resemblance was enough to make me back off slowly. I was unaware that Sonny had stopped working, and had walked over beside me. I almost jumped out of my skin when he spoke.

"So you don't like those suckers either huh?"

I stared at him for a few seconds, gathering my thoughts. "Sonny. This is going to sound really stupid. Here I am, having only just met you, and I am going to say something that will make you think I am nuts. I saw a couple of things that looked a bit like that just a few weeks ago. Scared the bejesus out of me. Just seeing these brought back memories I would rather forget."

"Scared the shit out of me too! I saw things like that

when I was 13. Woke up one morning and there they were, sitting on the end of my bed. Faded from view as I looked at 'em." He looked at me and I nodded to let him know it was similar in my case. "I was adopted. My adopted mum was OK, but the old man was an evil bastard. He'd just beaten the crap out of me a couple of days before that, and I was recuperating in bed. When I saw those things, sure got me out of bed in a hurry. I had no idea what they were. Still don't. No one believed me, but I saw them. I called them the Evil Ones."

I nodded again, in agreement. I also thought what an apt name. They seemed extremely evil themselves, and both of us had seen them after being in the presence of evil: in my case a gang that prided itself on being evil to the point that they adopted evil as their name. There are so many things in this world we do not understand. Most things I don't understand fascinate me and I love to discover..... but these things I hope I never see or have anything to do with again.

"I ran away from home a few days after that. Figured if I didn't, I'd kill that evil bastard next time he took a belt to me. I've never seen then since, but I associate them with evil. Funny thing is, I have always refused to make gargoyles even though people seem to like them. But, some rich dude in the city commissioned me to make him a half dozen unique ones. Gargoyles are ugly little bastards, supposed to ward off evil. To me, they are evil themselves. But,I was not about to turn down a five thousand dollar commission. I did the best I could to recreate what I saw. The guy loves em. I'm delivering them tomorrow. Good riddance as far as I'm concerned. Sight of them still makes me uncomfortable, even today. You are the first person I have ever met that admits to have seeing them also...although I bet others have and just don't want to sound foolish"

"Sonny. You did a damn good job of recreating! No one could catch the essence of evil they project, but you sure caught the basic look." Was a few months ago I saw them, but those statues still make me feel uncomfortable."

"Come with me Dave." He walked away from me, leaving the evil things behind, and opened a fridge. He reached in and pulled out two cold beers. "Probably too early for you., but when I am working over the fire, these things just seem to evaporate in my hand. I swear if my dick caught on fire I would not be able to raise enough spit to put it out. Besides, there's nothing like a beer to get your mind off bad thoughts." He thrust a beer into my hand, which I accepted gladly. He was right. His did seem to evaporate. One gulp and it was gone. "Gotta get back to work Dave. Have to finish this today. You wander round, we'll talk again. Think you and I are going to be good friends." He went back to his fire.

I wandered around for a few more minutes, left the empty by the fridge, and headed back out through the curtain. Cleo, who had been keeping me

company, ambled over to lay beside Sue. I waved to
Sue as I went out the door.

"See you soon Dave!" she yelled at me as I walked
out.

I found myself muttering to myself as I walked on.
"DAMN. I'm gonna like this town."
 I kept walking all the streets, checking out every
store I came to and familiarizing myself with the
layout of the residential streets. Without exception,
everyone was friendly. Just before lunch, I came to a
store called "Needful Things" Under the name was
a line that said "Proprietor, Steven King" Now that
was a store name and owner name made for each
other! I opened the door and a young athletic
looking guy looked up from his computer. " Hi. Be
with you in a second. Feel free to look around"

I did just that. The store was full of collectibles:
stamps, coins, comic books, dolls, rocks, fossils,
vinyl records an impressive collection of Sue's pots,
and a plethora of just about everything else in the
back half of the store. A person could spend hours in
a place like this.

"Hi. I'm Steven. Looking for anything in particular,
or just browsing?"

"Hi Steven. I'm Dave. I've just moved to town.
Opening a gym in the old feed store, and thought I
would walk around and introduce myself. Love your
store...and the name!"

Steve smiled. " Glad to meet you Dave. I'll be a customer. Friend of mine owns a store next to you. Sonny. Have you met him?" I nodded. "I've tried working out with him, but the man is just too intimidating for someone my size. I don't mean he means to intimidate. But damn. I struggle to bench 245 lbs, and he warms up with twice that much!"

"Steve, I know what you mean. the man intimidates me.... and that is a first for me. Is your name really Steven King?"

"Yea. I've lived here all my life. My dad was a stamp dealer back in the days when everyone collected stamps. I inherited his stock when he died, and when I opened a store to sell collectibles, just couldn't pass up on a chance to cash in on the famous Stephen King! He spells his name differently, but hardly anyone notices.... and it sure does catch attention. I'm not like Leland Gaunt in the famous book Needful Things. That guy was intent on destroying his town. This is a really friendly town, and I want it to stay that way. Besides, I sell mostly on line these days."

I'll come back and browse sometime Steve. See you don't sell any books? They are one of my passions. See you do sell Sue's pots though..."

"Oh yea. Love her work! Sell those mostly to tourists who have to come in when they see the store name. I don't sell books because Dawn has that market covered. You'll find her a few doors down."

Thanks Steve. I'll come back when I have more time."

'You got it....and I'll drop in as soon as you open."

Right next door to 'Needful Things' was a small restaurant. I stopped for lunch. Good food, well made, and reasonably priced. What city folk see in those chain restaurants I'll never figure out. My stomach felt really good as I left. That feeling was nothing next to the feeling I was about to experience for the first time.

CHAPTER 18

Next door to the restaurant was the town's used bookstore, with the catchy name of 'Your Local Bookie.'

I've mentioned the feeling I get when I am near a psycho. Extremely unnerving. Unique. Unpleasant. As I walked through the door of 'Your Local Bookie' and the lady behind the counter looked up and smiled, I experienced a feeling for the first time. Extremely unnerving. Extremely unique for me. Extremely pleasant. I doubt it was universally unique. Most of you have probably felt something like it....but it was new to me. My heart started to pound. I suddenly knew what people meant by love at first sight, a concept I had always scoffed at. I had known lots of beautiful women, and had certainly experienced lust at first sight many, many times before..... but this was like nothing I could have imagined. I must have stood staring at her a little too long; soft blonde hair, emerald green eyes framed by dark lashes, flawless cream coloured skin, exquisite lips. The picture of perfection. My idea of perfection. It was not just the obvious beauty. She could have been quite plain and I would have stared. There was something else totally indescribable , totally impossible for me to resist. I stared. Obviously I stared too long. The eyes took on a slightly wary look. I started to feel foolish.

"May I help you?"

"Damn. Sorry. I did not mean to stare. No matter how I say this, it is going to sound like a pick up line..." I paused for a second. "You don't know me, but if you did, you would know that nothing flusters me. Nothing. Well. Nothing did, until I opened that door. God, I feel stupid saying this. I felt an instant attraction. Felt like I've known you all my life. Never felt that before. Totally, totally threw me. That is why I was staring. Want me to go back out, come back in and be my usual cool self?"

Dawn actually blushed. Then smiled again. "That won't be necessary. I understand. I have experienced Deja Vu. But, I think if I had met you before, I would remember.... Now that I have met you, what can I do for you? Anything particular, or just browsing?"

"Actually, I just moved to Beaver Valley. I'm just going around town seeing what is here, and introducing myself, and in your case, making a fool of myself." I smiled. "My name is Dave. I just bought the old feed store, and in a month or so will be opening a gym there. Started off at Sonny and Sue's, and have been checking out the entire town. Actually, Sue said you are pretty good at aerobics. I'm putting aside 700 feet for that. Maybe, once I get up and running we could talk? Meanwhile, if you don't mind, I'd like to browse a little...I'm an avid reader."
"We can certainly talk about that later. I enjoy

aerobics. Meanwhile, feel free to browse. There are a lot of books here. If you need help, let me know." She went back to her book. I started to wander.

I selected 4 books, two mysteries, two books on local flora and fauna. It was large by bookstore standards, and her selection was extensive and interesting. I even found one of my own books! I took my selections up to the counter.

"Good choices. I've actually read all of these myself. We have similar tastes. All good. You'll like them."

I put my book on the counter. "Have you read this one?"

"Yes! It is a delightful book. Have never been able to find anything else by the same author. Wish I could. Did you want to buy it? If you enjoy the outdoors and wildlife, I promise you, you will enjoy it."

"No, I won't be buying it, but the author has written a couple of other books in the same vein. I'll bring you a couple. I have lots. I wrote it. Was amazed to find it here."

She looked questioningly at me. "You wrote it? I thought you said your name was Dave?"

"It is. My last name is Death. I wrote this when I was 17. Figured no one would buy a book on nature from a guy named Death, so I used the pen name

Barry Tuddenham. Written a couple since. Hope to write a couple more once I get settled in here. Not big sellers.... but I have fun writing them."

"Dave, I am impressed! I meant it when I said it was a delightful book."

"Well, I can at least leave on a good note. After my embarrassing entrance, I can't expect to leave while I am ahead..... but hopefully I am at least even. Once again, my apologies. I'll drop back in a week or so with the others. Moving my parents here, and my books are at their old place. Right now, I better get on with my exploring. Was a real pleasure to meet you Dawn. More than I could ever have anticipated. I am sure it was a lot more pleasure for me than for you....but maybe I can change that with time."

I saw she blushed again slightly as I waved from the door.... but at least she was smiling again.

I visited every store, and walked every commercial street, and by the time I was finished, it was almost 5pm. I came across one other store that was of interest: a thrift store for a local cat sanctuary by the name of Cats Anonymous. Having volunteered for one before, I introduced myself to the volunteer behind the counter, an older lady. She spoke in glowing terms about the two women who had started Cats Anonymous. I told her I would have little time for volunteering, but hoped to help financially. That made her day! I know how difficult it is for such groups to raise funds. She gave me a brochure, and told me to check out the web site. I promised her I would.

I reckoned I just had time to drive back to Sonny and Sues to buy the pots I had my eye on, then have supper before I met Tom, the man Randy was sending over to apply for the job as my dad's assistant. I got to Sonny and Sue's just as they were locking up. I pulled in beside Sonny's Harley, got off and started to walk towards them, Sonny stared at my bike, and started to walk towards me. He moved closer, and let loose with a big, booming roar of laughter. It was not a demeaning laugh, but a genuine belly laugh of enjoyment. I could not help laughing myself at the same time as I asked what was so funny.

"*Hardly Davidson's*? I LOVE That! Recognized the writing script, but knew it couldn't say what it looked like. I ride a Harley 'cause I love to customize my bike, and because I don't fit on smaller bikes, but I have to admit I think the Japanese bikes are superior. I've been looking at the VStar 1300, which is actually more powerful than this baby, but did not want to give up the look. Now, I'm having second thoughts. Never thought of doing this. I love it!"

"I'm thinking of a 1300 myself. This old girl has seen better days. She was what I could afford when I had her built, but want to move up. Think Harleys are too expensive. Was thinking of getting a VStar, but would have to find someone around here to customize it for me. I'm useless at that myself."

"I'm your man there Dave. If you decide to get one, I'll do the work for you if you like. I did mine. Nothing I can't do with metal. You let me know what you want, and I'll do it. Might do one up for myself now that I have seen yours. Harleys are everywhere. How many people have a genuine 'Hardly'?" That booming, infectious laugh broke out again.

"I'll probably take you up on that. Right now, though, I see you are closing up. I came back to pick up a couple of your vases Sue. Want me to come back tomorrow? There is no rush."

"Hell no. Us pot dealers are always open for business." She grinned her infectious grin. You could not feel anything but happy around this two. Almost made me forget my disastrous meeting with Dawn. Almost. Not quite.

I knew which ones I wanted, so went over and picked them up quickly, so as not to hold them up. She told me a price that I knew was at least half of what I had seen at Needful Things. I told her so. "Yea, but we are neighbours. You get wholesale, same as Steve."

I packed the vases into my carrier, and was off for supper. Stomach satisfied, I went back to my room and started one of the books I had purchased..... but my mind kept drifting back to who I had purchased it from.

Tom showed up a few minutes before 7pm. He was not that big, but looked to be in good shape, and had an open, honest, intelligent face. We shook hands. I noticed his left hand was in a leather glove. I explained what I wanted. Explained that my dad was great at renovations and repairs of just about anything, but had problems with ladders and did not drive ...or at least had not driven in years. I explained that I reckoned the reason he didn't drive was he could not afford a car up until now, but that he blamed the leg. I explained that his economic situation had changed, and I saw no reason that he could not drive, but that he,Tom, would have to drive to start. I also explained he would be starting at a little over minimum wage, until he proved himself. But, if he did, as the business grew, we would look after him. So, the harder he worked, the faster the business got profitable, the better it was for everyone. I asked if he had any problems with that.

"No problems at all Mr. Death. Randy told me how to pronounce your name. I reckon Randy probably told you about this." He raised up the gloved hand. " I have what is known as a myoelectric prosthesis. Controlled by the electrical impulses all muscles produce. I've had it so long I can do almost anything a person can do with a real hand. Must admit, I've never used it to jerk off, but I probably could." He looked at me and grinned.

I laughed. "Yes, he told me about it. It's not a problem. But. If you ever decide to try it out for jerking off, success or failure, either way, keep the results to yourself ! And, my name is Dave. I think the usual response to being called by your surname these days is to say 'Mr Death is my father'..... but in this case, I can't say that. I know my dad will insist you call him Ken."

"Thanks Dave. Appreciate that. What I'm not sure of is whether Randy told you I quit school at 16. I'm not big like you. When this happened, kids used to poke fun at me. I was always in fights. I sent a guy to hospital once. I was always in trouble, usually on suspension. I quit school as soon as I could."
"Yes, he mentioned it. Also not a problem. When you have a name like Death, you know what it's like to be poked fun at. I was in trouble a lot in high school too. Fortunately for me, I never sent anyone to hospital" I could have said I did send someone to the morgue, but some things are best left unsaid. "You be honest with us, work hard, and we'll get along great. You want to start straight away?"

He did. I got him to jump on the back of my Hardly. His eyes widened. "Cool bike!" I took him over to the house I had bought for my parents. Gave him a set of keys. Told him to start with the workshop in the back, fixing up the old benches there, building any new ones he thought would be necessary,sorting out the tools, etc. Then I wanted him to look in the house and decide what he could do by himself. Gave him my number and told him to call if he needed me, and order anything from Randy that he needed. Told him I was leaving him in charge. He was the boss. He beamed. Nothing a 22 year old who has had a few tough breaks likes to hear more than that. I reckoned if there were going to be problems, best to find out right away. Drove him back to the motel. I had noticed he had ridden his bicycle over. He rode off, and I went in for a restless night thinking about Dawn.

CHAPTER 19

Next morning, I got up early and drove back to Hardrock. No way I was waiting all that time to give those books to Dawn. I'd pick them up now. Dad was at work. He had given his notice, but was serving out the last two weeks. Mum was home, and all excited about the upcoming move. She had given up her job at the restaurant she worked at, but had been told to leave straight away. I gave her one of the vases I had purchased. The hug I got paid me back tenfold. Then I took her out to lunch and we had a good time, a good talk. I told her how impressed I was with all the people I had met. I even told her about Dawn and the fool I had made of myself. She told me not to worry. Any girl would be flattered to be told what I had told her, as long as they realized it was not just a line. Besides she said, any girl would be crazy not to grab me up if they got the chance. I laughed and told her that as my mum she was just a little bit biased...... but I sure hoped she was right. I dropped her back home, grabbed the books, and told her I would be picking them up in just over a week. I headed back to Beaver Valley.

First thing I did was have a shower and change into my best clothes. Even went out and bought polish, and polished my boots. Then I walked into town, picking up a dozen red roses as I came to the local florist. Ah. The joy of small towns. Everyone knows everyone. She recognized me from yesterday, and remembered my name. I remembered hers was Rose. Hard to forget a florist named Rose. When I asked her to put the roses in my vase, she recognized it instantly.

"Oh, this is gorgeous. Its one of Sues. She does such beautiful work. Must be for someone special! Who's the lucky lady?"

Small towns. Everybody knows everybody, and everybody wants to know what everybody else is doing. I figured if Dawn wanted people to know it was up to her. Besides, I did not know if she would even accept the flowers after yesterday. So, I just smiled and said:

"Let's just say that beautiful as the roses are, they pale in comparison to the lady receiving them."

"Ah. Gallant as well as handsome. Well, whoever she is Dave, I meant it. I think she is a lucky lady."

"Thanks Rose. I just hope she feels the same way."

When I walked into The Local Bookie, Dawn had customers. I wandered around browsing until the store was empty. Soon as they left, I was up at the counter.

"Was thinking a lot last night, Dawn. Yesterday was not the first time I have made a fool of myself.

Nobody ever called me smart and got away with it. But, I realized it **was** the first time I cared. So, figured I should face it now, not wait for a week or so. I drove up to Hardrock this morning and got the books I promised." I dropped a half dozen copies of each of the books I had written on her desk. Then I put the vase with the roses beside them. "Already made it clear how I feel, so I cant really play cool. I wanted you to have these. I know you are a friend of Sue, so I am sure you have some of her works, but I did not see any in the store. I figured I'd give you one. I think they are gorgeous. Also, I'd like to take you out to dinner. I want to get to know you, and vice versa. I'm available any night, and would love to take you out this evening. I realize you are probably busy, so whenever you like. Also, I realize you might be involved. If so, if you're comfortable with it, I'd still like to take you to dinner and get to know you, as a friend, but would understand totally if you did not want to though. But, I'm sure hoping your not. I'll shut up now. Just had to get that all out." It did come out all of a rush. Where was the cool Dave I was used to? I realized that I would actually lose playing poker against this women. She had me.

I could see the colour rising in her face again, but she did not look upset. " Dave, I'm not involved with anyone, but I'm not sure I want to be. You don't need to feel foolish. I felt an attraction to you too, and that has never happened to me before when someone walked through that door. I talked to my friend Sue about you, and she said she thought you were very nice, and her opinion means a lot to me. I would like to go to dinner with you and talk. But Dave, it will just be talk, OK? I have not been on a date for over a year, so I am a little rusty, but even though a girl is not supposed to say she is, I am available on short notice, and supper tonight would be great!" She rewarded me with a grin.

Just then, more customers came through the door. "Great! Want me to meet you here at say 7pm? I'll leave where to you, as you know the area. Somewhere nice. I see you have customers. I'll get out of here."

"7 pm here will be fine Dave." I turned towards the door. "Dave?" I turned back. "You can't leave without signing your books!" I complied, signing as David Death, writing as Barry Tuddenham.

"See you at 7!"

I went and had my haircut, then went and washed the truck. I like motorcycles, but not everyone does. Most women are not comfortable being seen on chopped bikes, even if they are Hardly's. Then I had another shower. Wasn't taking any chances.

I got to The Local Bookies at a little before 7. Was amazed to see the vase and flowers I had given Dawn on display in the front window, beside a display of books. My books! Dawn had made up a sign saying " Books by local author." I was standing looking at them when a voice behind me startled me. "Could not help but notice your interest sir. I own the store, and can open for you especially if you wish to buy one."

There she was. The sight of her took my breath away. But then, we have now been married for some time and it still does. I guess that's just me. Lucky, lucky bastard that I am. "Before I purchase, perhaps I could take you out to supper and discuss them?"

"Best offer I've had all day."

Dawn directed me to a restaurant just outside town called "The Fireside." We both thoroughly enjoyed learning about each other. I learned that she had been married to a man that abused her verbally and physically, and that was why she had not been dating for some time. I learned that her parents had both died in an accident. I learned that she was a trained librarian, but had decided to open her own store when she inherited enough to make her dream a reality. I learned she shared my love for animals and nature. She learned about my childhood, my gambling past, my adventures in Steeltown, my luck in Vegas and California, my travels over the last few months. I told her almost everything. Some things are best left unsaid. We also both learned that we thoroughly enjoyed each others company. They had to kick us out when they closed.

I drove her back to her place, a nice bungalow on one of the nicer streets of Beaver Valley.

"Dave. I know a lady isn't supposed to do this on a first date. I know I said it would just be going out to talk. But, I was wrong. Now it's my turn to be feel foolish. You want to come in, for, er, coffee?"

She did not have to ask me twice. Did not get a coffee that night. She told me to be gentle, as it had been a while. Did not have to tell me that either. The night was incredible for both of us. In the morning, I got up early enough to make breakfast, and I made **her** coffee...in bed.

CHAPTER 20

I drove Dawn to work. Got out of the truck, went round to open her door and kissed her. "Pick you up when you close?" Her look told me everything. We have hardly been apart for more than 24 hours since that day, other than when my travelling made it necessary. I am, as I said, a lucky, lucky bastard.

I started my day arranging signs . I had decided on the name 'Paladin's Gym'. I didn't use the name anymore.....but I still liked it. Then I arranged gym contracts through the local lawyer, then arranged to have the gym carpeted. The ceiling was wide open to the rafters, so I decided to talk to Randy at the building centre about that. He suggested drop ceilings. He said we could install them ourselves, but he did not recommend it.... pros could do it in a tenth of the time it would take us. I trusted him. I took his recommendation, and arranged that too. At the end of the day, I dropped in to see how Tom was doing, and was amazed to find that he had the place cleaned up, the benches all repaired and built as necessary, and all the tools displayed on peg boards for easy location. Turned out he had been excited to start, and had arrived before day break. Told me he did not want extra....he just wanted to get it done. He also surprised me when he said he had been inspecting the house, and had experience sanding down wood floors. He'd worked a summer for a guy that did that. I told him there were two sets of floors to do... here and my farm outside town. He grinned and said he could have them done in two to three days. I was starting to realize I had a good man here. The two weeks flashed by. When I drove up to pick up mum and dad Friday evening, Dawn came with me, closing her store for the weekend. They hit it off right from the start. When we got to the house, my parents were both overwhelmed by the transformation Tom had provided so far. Once again there were tears in my dad's eyes when he saw the well stocked workshop and the truck I had bought for him. I explained to them that new furniture was on the way, along with new appliances, bathroom fixtures, etc..... indeed deliveries would be arriving all next week. Until then, they would have to make do.... but I knew that even before the renovations were finished,they had never had such a nice place to live. I told them to get an early night as we would be leaving bright and early the next morning on an important trip. Dawn and I left them and planned an early night ourselves. I didn't know about mum and dad, but I knew despite the early night, Dawn and I would not be getting to sleep early.

Next day Dawn and I first hooked up to the cargo trailer, then picked up Tom, then my parents. We drove to the best charity thrift store I had come across on my travels. On the way there, just as I expected, Tom was a hit with everyone. I had noticed his best clothes when he came to see me for the job, and they had obviously seen better days, so

I wanted him on this trip. The thrift store was run by a large charity, and was absolutely huge. Located close to a very wealthy neighbourhood, the quality of their donated goods was exceptional, and I had seen on my last visit that they were overflowing with far more donations than they could use. Prices were ridiculously cheap. I told everyone to grab their own cart and fill it up.... I did not want to see any wasted space in any cart by the time they were finished. Told mum she should look for pots and pans as well as clothes, as I had noticed the ones they had were far better than hers. She could fill two carts. I intended to stock up too. Last time I had been here I was on the motorcycle. This time I intended to fill a trailer! But I had business to attend to first. I would have loved to have shopped in Beaver Valley at the Cats Anonymous Thrift Store, but unfortunately, although their quality was far better than mum and dad had ever been able to get in Hardrock, it was not a touch on this store's quality. I had an idea to rectify that, and after shooing everyone off to shop until they dropped, I went in search of the manager. I discussed my idea with her, she thought it was great, and she provided me with a direct email contact for the directors of the charity. Then I joined everyone else stocking up. We did well.

On the way home, Tom wanted to know how he could pay for his finds. I told him to consider it his first bonus. Tom and my parents had talked on the way, and they had all agreed to work double time to get our two houses finished as quickly as possible.

Tom had done an amazing job on the floors.... they would be covered with cloths to prevent damage as everything else was seen to. Dawn and I dropped everyone off, and left them to get on with things.

Dawn and I went to a farmer's auction Sunday. Farm tractors can cost up to around $100,000. But I managed to buy an older, 1970's model and all the attachments I would need for under $2,000. Things were going fantastic. That was about to change.

CHAPTER 21

I had moved out of the motel, and was sort of staying in my travel trailer at the gym. I say sort of, because I was always at Dawn's .... but I left bright and early in the morning to get a full days work in fixing up what I could and waiting for deliveries.

I had just gone into the trailer to make coffee to kick start me when through the kitchen window I saw Sue arrive on her little motorcycle. I remembered that Sonny had said he was leaving that morning for a couple of days of delivery. I knew how she took her coffee by then, so figured I would make her one too and take it over. She had no sooner entered the building though and a van pulled up, and four guys got out. They looked around furtively, and did not see me. They made a rush for the door of Sonny and Sues. All of a sudden I did not need a coffee. I was wide awake. I had recognized one of them from the snake tattoo running up his arm. It was Snake of coitus interruptus fame at the Evil One's meeting! They had no sooner entered the building and closed the door behind them than I was out of the trailer and running faster than I thought was possible.

When I hit the door it flew open. One of the guys was just about to lock it.

"Fuck off ass-hole. This is a private meeting" he said, just before I hit him hard in the windpipe, following the punch up with a boot to the nuts and a viscous uppercut to his jaw as he doubled over. Unlike in the movies, people do not get up quickly from such an attack. Snake was over against the wall, pinning Sue there. He had torn her blouse off, and there was blood trickling down from where he had hit her in the mouth. He was using one hand to hold her, one to unzip his pants. I had already seen what he had in there. Was not impressed then, did not want to see it again. The other two guys came towards me, both with knives in their hands. Idiots. They should have spread out, taking me from two sides, but they came together as one. I rushed to greet them. One guy was a little faster than the other. As he got to me, he slashed with the knife, which cut my arm slightly, nothing serious. I grabbed his knife hand , snapped his arm at the elbow, and tossed him screaming into the arms of his buddy. His buddy had better luck with the knife, burying it deep, but unfortunately for both of them, in the side of his friend, not me. While he figured out what to do, I gave him a head butt to the nose, smashing it flat, and delivered an uppercut to the guy with the knife in his side. Neither of them would be getting up soon. Snake was another story. I now had his full attention. He had turned to me, gun in hand. I reckoned my only chance was to rush him. I knew he was going to get a shot or two off before I got to him, but could only hope they would not be fatal. Things did not look good. As a gambling man, I figured I would have had better luck trying to win the lottery....but I had no choice, and I had no time.

I had forgotten about Sue. So had Snake. As I watched the gun rising to aim at me the huge gaping mouth of the gun was the only thing I saw. Guns coming up in position to kill you have that effect. I was fixated, and was amazed to see it falling, followed by Snake. Sue had grabbed one of her pots and used all her strength to smash it into the back of his head. He staggered, surrounded by shards of pottery, dropped his arm, but did not drop the gun. He did not need to. As he started to recover and raise it again, I was on him. I kicked the gun from his hand and rattled his teeth from one side of his mouth to the other with a right and a left, followed by a head butt to the nose. His head and the other guys would make a nice pair of matching bookends if you liked that sort of thing .....

"You OK Sue?" I handed her her blouse.

"Oh God Dave. Oh God. Thank God you showed up, Dave!" Sue was obviously shaken, but seemed OK.

"Nice shot with the pot Sue. We'll go through the wallets on these guys in a bit, and they can pay for it. Retail." She actually managed one of her wonderful grins.

"I've never seen anyone fight like that Dave. Remind me not to get on your bad side." I grinned back. She said "I'll call the cops"

"No Sue. We can't do that. I recognized one of these guys as he got out of the truck. That's why I came running so fast. Not sure about the other three, but that ugly guy with the gun is a full patch Evil One from Steeltown." I paused, to take the time to go over to the guy by the door who was trying to stand up. I helped him lay down to sleep again for a while. The others were in no condition to move for a few minutes. " When you pick a fight with one of them, you've picked a fight with them all. If we call the cops, they'll throw them in jail, but first thing they will do is contact the club for bail, say what happened, and we'll have twenty or more of the bastards up here in no time. We don't want that." Sue started to look really worried again.

"Don't worry. I'll think this through. We can come out OK. What I want you to do is phone Sonny. Tell him you are OK, but you need him back. Don't tell him what happened, just say you got hurt, but are fine, you want him home. He wont have gotten far, and will be worried enough by that. I've got to tie up these guys and gag them to keep them under control while I think. But, I better patch up that guy with the knife in his side. Otherwise he'll bleed to death."

We both did what we had to do. While I was tying them up, I removed their jackets. Sure enough, they had their colours on underneath. Hard cores like them feel naked without their colours, but I guessed they had covered them to avoid problems if they were stopped by the cops for any reason. I took off their colours and tossed them in a pile on the floor. Took their wallets too, making sure I knew which one belonged to who.

"Sue. You feel up to going and getting us a couple of coffees? I need to sit and think." Sue said no problem. She just needed to wash her face. "Thanks Sue. Take your time. Walk down to the coffee shop." She looked at me and the slight smile told me she understood.

"I'll see you in about an hour Dave. Sonny said he was a little over an hour and a half into the journey.....but I reckon he'll be coming back faster." I reckoned so too. Sonny felt about Sue like I felt about Dawn.

First I took care of the knife wound. It did not look like it had done any serious damage, so I just bandaged it up. Later he could go to a hospital to get it cleaned and stitched. Then I threw a bucket of cold water on each of them. I dragged the one with the broken arm into the back area. I rummaged up some paper, and came to sit beside him. He did not look too happy to see me. Such is life. I had not received my warning chill with any of them, so they were not psychos ....but they were evil bastards. I wasn't going to kill them, but they weren't going to be happy with my means of getting information.

"Well. I see you used to be an Evil One. I say 'used to be' because I took your colours, and I'm keeping them. I know how this works. You go back after having them taken, and they are going to kick you out of the group at the very least. You know that being stripped of your colours is a serious problem. How serious depends on your president. Who is your president?" He did not answer. So, I asked him another question. I asked him if this hurt, and twisted his broken arm for him. He did not have to answer that question. The scream said it all.

"I don't like having to repeat myself. Takes too much time. I would answer me promptly after this if I were you. Oh. I would not lie either. I'll know when you do. So, tell me, who's your president?" He could not say Bullwhip fast enough. So, Johnny had made it all the way to the top.

"Good boy. We're communicating. That's good. Now, I happen to know a little about Bullwhip. I happen to know that he is a certifiable psychopath. I don't think Bullwhip will be too forgiving about you losing your colours, do you?" The look of terror as he thought of it told me he knew I was right.

"OK. Next question. This is to make my life easier. You do want to make my life easier, don't you?" He nodded. "I have three other wallets here. I have the names of everyone in that other room.... but I want their club names." He gave me three names. I must admit they sounded pretty convincing, but none of them was Snake, so I knew he was lying. I gave his arm another twist, and the scream was truly pitiful. But, this man deserved no pity.

"Tsk. Tsk. Told you not to lie. Now, why don't you tell me their names. I'll give you their wallet id.,you tell me their club name." This time he identified Snake correctly. I had no reason to believe he would lie about the other two and not that one. "So. One wallet left. Yours. Now, bearing in mind that each one of your buddies is coming in here for the same treatment as you, why don't you tell me your club name? Save me having to bring you back in to edit your story." It was heartwarming how eager he was to tell me.

Where do they get those names! "So, Magoo, I've got good news and bad news for you .The bad news is I know all about the 'all for one and one for all' biker code. You go back to Steeltown, say what happened here, and even if you lie and say ten guys took you instead of just little old me, the next thing you know I'm gonna have a whole bunch of scum like you to deal with. Believe it or not, I could handle it with a little help from my friends. But, I have a lot on my plate right now. I'd rather avoid that if I can. It would seem to me that killing you and dropping you in the local swamp would solve that problem. But, that could be a problem too. Little waves can become big waves.

So, the good news is, I have another solution. Now, bearing in mind that I am going to be bringing each one of your buddies in here, and each one is going to go through the same treatment that you have, I am going to need some answers from you. If you tell the truth, the truth will set you free. I know how much you will miss me, but I will set you free, on condition that you tell the truth and then I never, ever, see you again. I am going to verify what you say with your buddies. If I find out you are lying, I am going to introduce you to our local swamp. Do we understand each other?" He nodded.

"Now the first obvious question is, what the fuck were you doing here?" He told me that they had been ordered to bring back a pretty woman, and had seen Sue drive by and had followed her.
"Who told you to do that Magoo? Bullwhip?" He nodded.

"When I walked in here you were in the process of gang raping my friend if I am not mistaken. I know the cops would see it that way.....but I will not be telling them about this. You will either walk away never to return, or you will die. No cops. So, tell me, was this part of Bullwhip's orders?" He told me Bullwhip did not care if they had a little fun, as long as they brought the girl back in a condition that she could be sent out to earn money.

"By earn money, I assume you mean through prostitution and stripping operations, much the same as Bullwhips' predecessor, Nails, used to operate? Does he collect souvenirs the same way Nails did?" I could tell he was surprised that I knew about Nails and his methods of instilling terror into his victims. But, he nodded and confirmed that Johnny had learned well from his predecessor.
I let him sit there while I wrote out a short note

outlining what we had discussed.

"OK Magoo. If your friends confirm what you have said, you are a lucky man. You get to haul your ass out of my town to the nearest local hospital, get yourself fixed up, and head for parts unknown. All you have to do is sign this, with your real name and your club name. That easy." I had expected a little more persuasion would have been necessary, but he did as he was told without hesitation. I dragged him back further into Sonny's part of the shop, where he would not be able to communicate with the others, but could hear any screams that ensued, then went out and brought in number two. I brought in the guy with the stab wound, figuring he would be the easiest to hurt if needs be, but one little tap on his side was all that was necessary. The next guy agreed with the previous two confessions, and signed without so much as a moments hesitation. I saved Snake for last, figuring he might be more of a problem, but once I showed him the three signed confessions and explained that, seeing as how he seemed to be the leader, and therefore the most responsible, if needs be I would have no qualms disposing of him and letting the others go free. He listened to reason. It had gone easier than expected.

When Sue came back with coffees I had the guys back out in front, tied and gagged. I showed her the confessions. Then I went back to the four of them and explained that they could get their own coffees in a few minutes if they wanted. They just had to wait for my friends husband to show up, then they

187

could be on their way. I don't think they believed me at that point. I did not give a shit.

Sue and I went over to enjoy our coffees where we could talk without being overheard. Sue was amazingly tough, and was already settled right back down despite what she had been through, and despite what she read was to have been her fate. She confirmed that she had not told Sonny any details, only that four guys had broken in, and I had captured them. I outlined my plans. I had barely finished when the door burst open, and in Rushed Sonny. The man is so huge, he almost tore the frame off the door coming in. The look of rage on his face was enough to scare the hell out of me. When he looked over at the four guys bound and gagged, one of them actually crapped himself. I could understand that.

"What the hell happened Dave?" I asked him to go outside with Sue, and she would explain. Told him everything was under control. While they were outside, I explained to our guests that the man that had just come in was one of the friends that would help me clear up any future problems should they ever return. I also explained that he was not my largest friend, either. I had just called him in because it was his wife they had been messing with. I had lots of friends like that. Must be something in the water. I lied, but I actually think they believed me.

When Sue and Sonny came back in, the look of anger and hate on his face had not diminished, but he was under control. Obviously Sue had explained things as I had asked.

"Well my friend. These gentlemen have an urgent engagement elsewhere. Want to help me untie them and send them on their way?"

We untied Snake and the largest of the other three remaining, and Sonny picked them up off the floor, one in each hand. Sue opened the door, and he turned sideways and took them out, tossing them into the truck. I untied and took the other two out one at a time, starting with the guy that had messed his pants. I handled him very gingerly . He had really made a mess. But, there was no fear of him attempting to escape. He saw Sonny standing there and literally made a run for the back of the van and jumped inside. I don't think his friends were glad to receive him in his condition, but they had enough brains to keep their complaints to themselves. Then I brought the last guy out, along with the keys to the van and their wallets. I explained to them that I had taken enough cash out to pay for damages and clean up, but had left everything else as it was. I pointed down the road and explained there was a hospital about 20 miles down that way, suggested they tell the staff at the hospital that they had been fighting amongst themselves, and once they were released, suggested they just keep on going in that direction. The coast was another thousand miles or so. They peeled off as if they wanted to hit the coast the next day.
Sonny and Sue started to thank me again. I told

them to forget it. I knew damn well they would have done the same for me. I told them we could make everything better, but it would require some difficult decisions on our part. I was pretty certain from what I had heard from our guests that The Evil Ones were responsible for the mysterious disappearances that had been occurring all over the province. Sonny told me he would be more than happy to go down to Steeltown and kill them all. As a man who had killed more than once, I could tell he meant it. But I told them to go home, enjoy each others company and we would meet again tomorrow. They did just that. I recover much faster than most from such encounters. I decided, what the hell, just get on with my day

Vito called me soon after Sonny and Sue had left for home. Said he had all my equipment and could deliver it today if I wanted. I told him he could not have picked a better time; I had some favours to ask him. He said "Anything, my friend." When Vito said anything, he meant just that.

CHAPTER 22

When Vito arrived, I was pleased to see he had a
couple of grunts with him to help unload and set up
the equipment. Normally I would have helped; good
exercise. Today, I wanted to talk to Vito. I bought us
a case of beer and we retired to my office, to catch
up on news, and talk about my needs. Vito told me
that Johnny had taken over The Evil Ones, and if
anything, was worse than Nails. But, the problems
following Nails demise had seen their numbers
decimated. Some had ended up in jail, and some,
disillusioned with the outlaw life, had just drifted
away. Johnny was down to leading just fourteen
outlaws. I explained what had happened this
morning, and that now he was down to ten. Vito told
me that what I told him confirmed his suspicions:
Johnny was running girls again. He had been
puzzled that no girls seemed to be missing in
Steeltown, and no activity involving girls was
known to him there either. If he had not heard, he
was not surprised the cops did not know. They
thought they had solved the problem when they
cleaned house after Nail's death. But, Vito made it
his business to know what was going on in his town,
and had a guy he had brought in from the big city
that was prospecting with The Evil Ones at Vito's
request. Apparently the guy had told Vito that
Johnny had taken up one of Nail's old habits, and

was wearing what looked like fingernails in a necklace when he was at the clubhouse. Unlike nails, he never wore them where anyone that was not a member could see them. Vito's spy was disgusted with what he had learned so far, and wanted out, but Vito had asked him to stay until he found out where the girls were coming from, and where they were being kept. Vito knew where they were coming from now....but I needed him to keep his guy in place for just a little longer. I told Vito what I needed to know. He told me not a problem...would take him a couple of weeks, a month at the most. Another thing about Vito. When he said not a problem, he meant it. So few people do. Vito and I would never be friends, but we understood each other, and as I have mentioned before, he felt indebted and would do whatever it took to honour any request I made. Not for the first time I was thankful that I was on his good side. I would feel pity for anyone that was not..... well, almost anyone. I felt no pity for Johnny at all.

Vito and I had had a liquid lunch. His guys had worked right through the lunch period and had everything done by 5pm. Vito had promised them a $200 bonus, and a nice supper. Never seen guys work so hard. Probably had something to do with the bonus, but I suspect it had more to do with keeping Vito happy. Talking of happy, we were both that. Vito said goodbye and climbed into the truck to sleep it off, one of his guys driving. I decided the best thing for me to do was leave my truck and walk over to 'The Local Bookie' The walk over would sober me up some, and Dawn would understand once I explained what had happened today.

Understand would be an understatement. Sue was by far and away her best friend. The first thing Dawn did was give me a coffee, lock up the shop early, and phone Sue. When she got off the phone she said that I was her hero.... and Sonny's and Sue's. I deserved a hero's supper. She took me home and gave me my favourite meal. Then we went and sat outside and watched the sun go down. Later, she gave me a hero's welcome in bed.

Next morning, Dawn insisted on coming with me to meet Sonny and Sue. My truck was still there, unharmed. There is little crime in Beaver Valley, and I had been fairly certain that our friends would not return. I would be surprised if they were not halfway to the coast by now.

Thought Sonny was going to crack one of my ribs, the bear hug he gave me. He said he was horrified at how close he had been to losing Sue. That and the thought of it happening to others still had him in a murderous rage. I told them of my visit from Vito. Explained that involving the cops could have serious repercussions for everyone, ourselves included. If no one knew where the girls were kept, chances were the cops would not find out either, and the operation would go underground even further. What the girls had gone through, indeed were still going through, was nightmarish, but we could be fairly certain that without anyone knowing where they were kept, Johnny would just kill them all. There was a good chance he would get away with it. We could be certain that enough information would become public that we would be exposed. We could count on retaliation, and it would not be pleasant. Unless we provided the confessions I had obtained, we had little to offer in the way of proof or evidence. If we provided the confessions, we would have a lot of explaining to do ourselves. I am afraid I had little confidence the police and the judicial system would be able to see justice was done. There were just so many cases where investigations resulted in no meaningful result. Last but not least, I had given my word I would not pursue the four we had let go. Scum that they were, going back on my word was not something I did. I was pretty sure that away from The Evil Ones, whilst they would never become model citizens, we could be pretty sure they would not be anywhere near as destructive to normal life as they had been.

We would have to deal with things ourselves, and we could not do that until I heard back from Vito. It was hard knowing nothing could be done to help those girls or to punish those involved, but in the real world it is not possible to solve all problems quickly and easily. Hard as it was, we had to wait. They understood. Sonny said he would do anything. Anything, to stop their operation, indeed their existence. Dawn and Sue both said that no matter what had to be done, they understood. I would never tell them what had to be done; some things are best kept to yourself. But it was nice to know they understood in the abstract.

We continued as before, only perhaps more so. You can either sit and brood while you wait, or get involved with activities at an even more frantic pace than usual. The latter is always the best choice. We agreed to keep everything amongst ourselves, not to be discussed in any way, even with our closest friends. That was not too difficult, as even though the time had been short, we are all each others closest friends already.

Although we all kept busy all hours of the day and most of the night, I know the time dragged for all of us. Knowing that there were women being held as slaves and living in terror is a hard thing to live with when you are helpless to do anything about it. Knowing that Sue had almost been one of them heightened the feelings. Although we were working at a frenzied pace to make the time pass, we tried to keep our set routines going as normal. Since we all got along so well, we had begun meeting at my farm house for a poker night each Friday. I had a huge kitchen table ideal for the purpose. There were anywhere from 4 to 8 players every Friday. Sonny and Sue always came, sometimes my mum and dad did, and sometimes Steven and Anne. I had explained to them how I had made my fortune, and how I no longer played for money, especially with friends. So, we played to see who would pay for breakfast for us all the next morning. I refused to deliberately lose hands, but explained that I would not bet properly, to ensure that I did not end up a winner every time. I did explain to them what they were doing wrong when they made mistakes, and explained how an observant player could read what an unsuspecting player was holding by studying tells. Over time they would all become excellent players, except for Sonny. His face showed every emotion and he seemed incapable of hiding them. It was a good job he was so talented, and his work was in such high demand. He ended up paying for a lot of breakfasts!

CHAPTER 23

Sunday Dawn and I went out to visit Cats Anonymous. Tish and Jody were a treat to meet. They both believed strongly in what they were doing and spent seven days a week doing it. I thought Tish had a cold when she started to talk, but it turns out she has an allergy to cats! She said it was no big deal. She took antihistamines, and the sniffles would clear up later.... was just an annoyance first thing in the morning. It spoke volumes about her dedication.

Cats Anonymous is all volunteer. I found out they were constantly broke as they spent more hours looking after the cats than most people spend on making a living. They survived personally by doing a variety of part time jobs, pet sitting, in house nail trimming, etc. Yet, loving what they did, they were obviously far happier than the majority of people who spend most of their time chasing money; they always seemed to find enough to keep food on the table. Food in the bowls for the sixty odd cats they had on hand, not counting the dozen that were their own house cats, was a different matter. That came mostly from donations from pet food manufactures, pet stores and volunteers.

Some people that are horrified by the callous way

people just discard cats at the first little inconvenience end up taking in hundreds, and are laughed at by society , labeled crazy cat people. I can understand why they do it: it's hard to say no when it seems the only alternative for a cat is a life on the mean streets of humanity, but Tish and Jody realized that this was a recipe for disaster, and kept the population down to a manageable sixty or so in the shelter. That number could be properly cared for by them and their dedicated volunteers until a forever home was found. They knew they could only do so much against the seemingly endless, horrendous tide of discarded pets. Tish told us the story of the little boy on the beach:

"A little boy was standing at the seashore, picking up starfish that had washed up on the beach, and tossing them back into the sea. Curious, a man passing by asked him what an earth he was doing. 'I'm saving the lives of these starfish mister' The man laughed contemptuously. 'That's ridiculous. Look, there are thousands upon thousands. You can't throw them all back in. All your efforts will make no difference.' The little boy continued what he was doing. 'I would not say that mister. I know I can't save 'em all, but what I am doing sure makes a hell of a difference to the ones I toss back!'

We told them we were actually more dog people than cat people, and wanted to find a couple of dogs to adopt, but we would love to adopt a couple of cats now if we could, cats that would be ok with big dogs. Turned out Tish and Jody had a couple of dogs also, so they understood. Like us, all pets, all animals were important to them. They knew the personality of each and every cat in their care, and introduced us to Bijou and Zoe, two adorable black cats, each about 4 years old. They had come from a home with a couple of dogs, and got along great with them. Tish figured they would be perfect for us, and explained: "You will need to fill out our adoption questionnaire. We strive to match up the right cat with the right family, and to ensure that our cats are adopted into homes where they will be a part of the family, forever. We firmly believe that there is the right home for every cat, and the right cat for every home. By identifying your needs and lifestyle, and matching you up with the cats that fit those criteria, we are more likely to have a happy, successful adoption." Dawn asked why the people had given up such lovely girls. Tish sneezed, apologized, then laughed. "the lady of the house suddenly decided she was allergic to cats!" We all laughed at the irony of Tish having to accept that as an excuse. I said I hoped she sneezed in the woman's face when she was giving them up!

We also wanted to volunteer to help at the shelter, Sundays if possible, as we both worked other days. We explained that we could not start for a few weeks as I was pushing with everything I had to open the gym. I also asked if they would be willing to come with us on a trip to the big city. I saw the puzzled look, and explained the reason was a surprise, but promised it would be more than worth their while. Indeed, if they could make it tomorrow,

that would be great: Dawn's store was closed
Mondays. Still seeing hesitancy, I assured them I
would not be taking time off to take the trip myself
if I did not think it was important.... I guaranteed
them it would be exciting for them.

"You really have us curious now. See you at 9am?"
Told them we would pick them up. We left with
Bijou and Zoe, eager to introduce them to their new
forever home. Told them we would return the
carriers tomorrow.

*(for more information on Cats Anonymous, please visit their
web site, www.catsanonymous.ca)*

CHAPTER 24

Monday we picked them up, four large coffees already purchased, ready for the road. I was pulling the cargo trailer. The trip was a great chance to get to know each other, and we became good friends. They kept asking what this was all about, we kept ignoring the question. When we got to the thrift store we had recently visited, I told them I wanted the trailer stuffed with as much as they could get in it.... it was all paid for, and I wanted them to restock their thrift store with the best they could find. Never saw two people enjoy shopping so much! Told them that whenever they needed more, all they had to do was ask, and I would drive them down for a load. I had arranged to buy from the thrift store at wholesale whenever they needed to. In fact, after seeing their reaction, told them I was going to do the same thing for the thrift store I volunteered at while I was in Steeltown.

Tuesday, hard at it trying to make up for lost time, I was a little annoyed to be interrupted by a knock at the door. Was some guy wondering if I was going to vote for him in the countries upcoming election. I told him that I did not vote. One party was as bad as the other. He said that well, if I did not vote, I could not complain. I told him I had heard that so many times, and it always struck me as a crock. It was like telling me I could not participate in a discussion of sports unless I held season tickets to the games. If all the teams were lousy, I had every right not to support any of them, and every right to bitch about their lousy performance. Told him I felt that way about all governments. Our governments are corrupt, and the system is broken. Things had deteriorated so far since Lincoln said in the Gettysburg Address 'government of the people, by the people, for the people', that we now had government of big business, by big business, for big business. He countered by saying that our system of government may not be perfect, but was the best there was, and he was the best candidate. I said that was a crock of shit also. I reckoned anyone could come up with a better system if they took the blinders off , looked around and thought about it. Then I told him a joke.

"A small boy is given an assignment in school to write an article on politics. So, he goes and asks his father: 'Dad. What's politics?'
'Well son. If this is for school, you have to put it in your own words. But, I'll explain by giving you things to think about. I bring home the money for this family to live on, so call me Capitalism. Your mum runs the family, so she is the Government. Your nanny works hard, and makes a small wage, so call her the Working Class. You are the People, and your baby brother is the Future. Think about how this family all works as a unit.'
The boy goes to bed, but wakes up around two am to hear his brother crying. He calls out to mum, but gets no answer. So, he goes to look at the baby, and

can smell that he needs his diaper changed. He goes to fetch his mum, but she has taken a sleeping pill and will not wake up. He goes to find his nanny, but when he opens the door, there is his dad on top of the nanny. The boy goes back to bed and covers his head with a pillow so that he can sleep. In the morning he goes and talks to his father.

'Dad, I think I understand politics.'

'Great son! Explain it in your own words'

'OK. While the People are being ignored, the Government sleeps and does nothing, and Capitalism screws the Working Class. Because of this, the Future is in deep shit.'"

I could tell the guy was getting a little upset. I apologized for being so abrupt, and explained that I was up to my ears in work. He said the reason I could work was because of our great system, and he doubted anyone could come up with a better one. I told him I would try and think of a better system while I worked, and if he wanted to come back tomorrow I'd give him what I came up with.... and if I could not come up with something, I would vote for him. That made him smile, and he assured me he would be here. I assured him I would be too.

It was great to have something to think about, to take my mind off those women. When I got home, I had the gist of an idea, and Dawn and I sat out on the porch thinking it through.

Sure enough, he showed up, expecting I suspect to hear that I would vote for him. I explained that , whilst I was certainly no expert, I had figured out what I thought would be a better system in a few hours. I was sure there were flaws in it, but I looked forward to hearing what they were if he came up with them. I figured if someone as non political as I could come up with ideas in such a short period of time, surely great political minds could come up with a hell of a lot better.... but I doubted they would because the big businesses that really called the shots would not let them. He said he would study it and tell me the problems with it.... but he never came back again. If nothing else, it was a great way to get rid of him I guess.

(for David's political views, see page 244)

CHAPTER 25

Wednesday evening, when Dawn answered the doorbell, it was Tish and Jodie's turn to surprise us. Each was carrying a young puppy with floppy ears and a big tail. Between them, they had eight of the biggest paws I have ever seen on puppies. Love at first sight. Dawn asked "They are adorable!What kind of mix are they?"

Tish laughed. "These are no mix,lady! These are purebred dobermans with ears and tails intact, as they should be. Brother and sister, they were rescued by friends of ours at the Humane society. No papers, but they are purebreds. You said you liked big dogs. These guys are going to be huge. Their dad was 140 lbs and their mum was over 100, and no fat on either of them. We met both the parents at the shelter, and they were both gentle and intelligent dogs. These guys are yours if you want them."

"Want them? You guys just **try** taking them away now that you have shown them to us! I can take them to the bookstore with me. I know dobermans need lots of human interaction, and are one of the most intelligent and loving dogs if treated correctly. Any customers that don't like it are welcome to leave!"

We cracked a bottle of wine to celebrate. Tish and

Jodie introduced these new editions to Bijou and Zoe. I can't say they were impressed with the new additions, but they tolerated them. The two dogs went exploring under our watchful eyes. Dobermans walk mostly on their toes rather than their pads like other dogs do, so their nails clicked on the floor as they walked around. Dawn said " Wow. You may have to marry me Dave .We have only been together a couple of weeks, and already we have the pitter patter of tiny feet around the house. Well, actually not so tiny." I grinned and said nothing would make me happier. Dawn grinned back. Hmmm. I said that was something we would have to discuss once the next week or so was over. For now, we cracked another bottle to toast the idea.... found out Tish and Jody really liked their wine! I explained I made my own beer and wine usually, and would be doing so as soon as I got the gym rolling. Tish said they would house sit our pets whenever needed. "Our new motto: Will work for wine and beer!"

Except for the Friday poker game, I had hardly seen Sonny and Sue. I was working long hours, but they were in their shop whenever I arrived, and the bike was still outside when I left. I figured if they were that busy, I should leave them alone. Had enough to keep myself busy anyway. But,Thursday afternoon, I found out why . Sue opened up the gates to the back storage area and Sonny drove out in his delivery ambulance, the big diesel growling as he pulled a heavy object behind it. Behind the ambulance was the most magnificent sculpture I think I had ever seen of a man holding a women up in the air. It was incomprehensible to me how anyone could make anything so beautiful, so detailed, from twisted pieces of steel.

"Dave. This scrap metal is taking up too much space in my backyard. Mind if I dump it in front of your building?" Both of them were grinning like a toothpaste ad. "This is our way of saying 'thank you.'"

"Sonny! That is absolutely gorgeous!! I just can't believe it! Thank you!"

"Don't thank me. Thank Sue. It was her idea, her design, and she helped me build it. I just put it together." I gave them both big hugs. Or, to be more precise, I gave Sue a big hug, and Sonny just about crushed me in his embrace.

I stepped back and said "I've gotta go!" They looked at me enquiringly. "I've gotta go get Dawn. She has to see this! Now!" I jumped in my truck and tore off. I looked back and they were still doing impressions of the Cheshire Cat from Alice in Wonderland. Actually, I felt like I had somehow landed in Wonderland. Apart from the awful images of the women that I knew were being held captive, images that just would not go away, I had never been so happy in my life as I was in Beaver Valley.

When I told Dawn she had to close up shop for a half hour, she never questioned. She could tell from my face I was excited about something. So much for my poker face. We each picked up a dog and got back in the truck. She was as ecstatic as I was when she saw the sculpture. Then it was her turn to hug Sue and be crushed by Sonny. We introduced our new family members, King (of farts) and Queen (of hearts), then, as Dawn had to get back to her store, we decided that we would take them out to supper Friday instead of our usual card game. Little did I know then it was a date we would not be able to keep.

(for information on Doberman's see page 246)

CHAPTER 26

Vito phoned me that evening. Everything I needed was accomplished. I spent half an hour on the phone with him. Ended saying I looked forward to seeing him tomorrow. Dawn knew what the call was about, so there was no surprise when I told her I had to leave for a few days. I phoned Sonny, so he could tell Sue the same. We would be leaving early in the morning for Steeltown. Told him to pack a change of clothes, some sweaters, and a raincoat, just in case. We would be outdoors a fair bit.

Dawn and I went to bed early, and made love. Afterwards, she held my head in her hands, looked into my eyes, and told me that anything I had to do was OK with her. Anything. Nothing else had to be said. The agonizing wait was over. Slept better than I had for weeks.

Was up early, and kissed Dawn goodbye, gym bag packed with the clothes I would need. It was the first time we had been apart since we met. I told her I was going to really miss her. She told me to hurry home so we could discuss that idea that had come up when Tish and Jody were over. That indeed gave me something to look forward to. I loaded my Hardly in the back of the cargo trailer, and picked up the few special things I had prepared for this trip.

I had explained to Sonny that Vito was an unusual man to say the least, but I trusted him totally. Then I told him what my plans were. Told him I would need him for some of what needed to be done, not for all if he did not want to. I would understand. Told me that no way I was keeping him out of it. That look of fury came back into his face as he said that. I knew damn well I would never want to have Sonny mad at me!!

First thing we did was meet with Vito. Vito was a cautious man, and he had not wanted to tell me too much over the phone, just that he had what I required. His man had found out the location of the holding house, had determined that Johnny was living at the club house now as there was a place there for the president, and had determined that there was a meeting and party there every Friday night. Johnny stayed 'home' afterwards, but all the rest usually left around two AM, usually in typical biker gang formation. I gave Vito the number on my throw away phone to give to his man, and Vito gave me the mans number. We did not need to meet. Was better we did not. Vito's man knew what I wanted him to do Saturday. Sonny and I said our goodbyes and went out to do some exploring. Vito wished us luck. With a little luck this whole thing would be over Saturday afternoon. Fingers crossed.

CHAPTER 27

Midnight found us on the road to The Evil Ones clubhouse. It had started to rain. That made it a little uncomfortable, but actually would help in what we had planned. We had found a spot ideal for our purposes. Sonny took one side of the road, I the other. We ran a clothes line that I had sprayed matte black across the road, one end to a thick tree on my side, one to the same on Sonny's . Apart from Evil Ones, traffic on the road was almost non existent, especially at night. Now we waited. I don't know what Sonny thought of. Probably revenge. I thought about Dawn.

Sure enough, a little after 2 am we heard the sound of chopped Harleys firing up. Most o them had straight pipes, so they were easy to hear, even though we were some distance off. They were about to learn an important lesson: if you are going to be an evil bastard and hurt a lot of people, best not to maintain routines and rituals. Payback is a bitch.

Outlaw motorcycle clubs pride themselves on their riding ability. Even when they were drunk and stoned as these guys surely were, they always rode in formation when in a group. And, they pride themselves on how tight they can ride together. Two abreast, and each pair right on the ass of the one in front. The most senior members always ride at the front. That suited our purposes also...they would be the ones to get hurt the most. Really did not want to kill them, but if it happened, it happened. Soon we saw 10 headlights coming towards us. We yanked up the rope, and tied it to the trees, at a height that would catch the front forks of the lead bikes, not the riders themselves.

The crash was spectacular! In the rain, the two lead riders never even saw the rope. It snapped on impact, but not before it sent those two flying over the handlebars doing face plants on the asphalt and sliding an impressive distance on the rain soaked road. Their bikes slid sideways making a barrier that all the others crashed into. I should have brought a flash camera!

We untied the rope, wound in the pieces, and met back at the truck. We figured one of them would manage to crawl back to the clubhouse. Johnny was not going to be pleased, and the hospitals would be very busy indeed tonight.

I had been afraid that Sonny would be upset, but his angry look had been replaced with a viscous grin. "Damn. That felt good. Those bastards got just what they deserved. I started to worry less about what tomorrow was to bring. Looked like Sonny would be able to handle it just fine.

We went back to our motel room. Slept the sleep of the just.

CHAPTER 28

Saturday, Vito's man was to go out and see Johnny and tell him he knew who had ambushed his men! Was to say he was someone he dealt with, someone that did not know he was prospecting for The Evil Ones. Someone who he had conned into meeting him that very afternoon. Did Johnny want revenge? Does a bear shit in the woods? He had been told to tell Johnny that the man he knew was a cautious type. He would phone him when he arrived at the meeting point. Johnny would have to hide his bike...Vito's man would say he had picked a spot that suited the purpose well. He would arrive in his truck so the guy would not be suspicious, and they would put Johhny's bike in a concealed spot that was ideal. Then they would go inside and wait. To make it sound convincing, Vito's man told Johnny he wanted five thousand dollars for setting it up. I was certain Johnny would agree to that, just as certain as I was that if it came time to pay up, Johnny would double cross the guy.... but I was banking on him not having to pay anyway.

I was pretty sure it would work, but Vito's man would phone me if there was a problem. No phone call came, so we headed for the rendezvous. Sonny was in the truck, I was on my Hardly.

The rendezvous selected was our old breakfast joint, Frank's. Wide open in all directions, just in case one of the riders had survived the crash enough to lay in ambush, but I doubted that. There was a barrier beside the restaurant to hide the garbage bins. That was where Johnny was to hide his bike. There were a number of cars in the parking lot. Franks was popular for brunch on Saturdays. I wanted people around. I was pretty sure Johnny would be packing a gun, and I did not want him using it there. I parked the bike a little way down the road, and jumped in with Sonny. Sonny drove around to the back of the barrier, and sure enough Johnny's bike was there. It only took me a few seconds to do what I had to, then Sonny drove me back to pick up my Hardly. He drove the truck back to sit amongst the other cars in the lot, and I drove my Hardly into the parking lot and phoned Vito's man on my throwaway.

Johnny was out the door in just a few seconds. I think he recognized the Hardly before he recognized me.

"You, you bastard!!!" He raced to get his bike. I took off down that road we had enjoyed so much in the past, in a life that seemed so alien to me now. I heard the roar of his chopper, but did not look around. I knew Sonny would follow in the truck, and I knew Vito's man would order brunch and flirt with the waitress, to ensure his alibi was rock solid should he need one. His work was done. I just hoped he did not get to try and collect his reward!

I had a pretty good lead, but could tell Johnny was gaining on me. I guess I had gotten a little more cautious, and/or Johnny was a little more reckless. I knew he desperately wanted to kill me, and that spurred him on, just like it spurred me to push a little more than I would have liked.

When the explosion occurred, Johnny was right on my tail going into one of the S curves, both of us with our foot pegs digging into the asphalt as we leaned over hard.

I slowed and turned in time to see his chopper cartwheeling across the bog, and splashing into the river, where it disappeared, roiling the water up as it sank. Johnny was doing the most amazing dance, one moment almost standing and whacking into the stumps of dead trees, at other times sliding face first through the swamp. I could see mists of blood appear each time he contacted something particularly hard. He finally came to rest, face up, several hundred feet from the road, and his body almost disappearing into the ooze. Sonny drove up and we made our way through the swamp. I had an untraceable gun Vito had given me, but was hoping I would not have to use it, hoping the death could seem like an accident. When we got close, we could see the malevolence in his one remaining eye. One had been torn out in this trip to his final resting place, along with the ear on the same side. He was not speaking. Would have been hard: most of his teeth were gone and his mouth was torn across his cheek. Looked like he had also torn his femoral artery.... the ooze all around him was stained red. As we watched, the light in his remaining eye went out, and he gradually slipped totally into the mire. I was reminded of that scene in Terminator 2, where the cyborg disappears into the molten metal. Come to think of it, that was called Terminator 2: Judgement Day. Fitting. Sonny looked at where Johnny had been, spat, and said it was a fitting end for a piece of slime...back into the ooze he came from. I knew Sonny was going to be alright with it. I tossed the throw away gun into the river...would not need it. I looked like an accident, but I would be surprised if they ever found him My last thought as we turned away was that I had been wrong, and Johnny right. I had constantly been warning Johnny in our earlier days about the dangers of steroid use. Turned out, as he thought, he had not needed to worry about that at all.

In case you are wondering about the explosion, I'll tell you a little about it. If you put liquid Draino in a plastic bottle, along with a few other ingredients I will not tell you, then drop it in a gas tank, the gas will eat the plastic away. When the two mix, BOOM! You can even time the explosion fairly accurately by using the correct thickness of plastic. You may have heard that sugar in the tank will cause the engine to seize. Not really true. Gums up the engine, but difficult to tell when it will stall...and it rarely seizes.

We put the Hardly in the back of the trailer, and headed back to the motel for a shower. On the way, I used the burner phone to call the police and tell them where the women were being held. Those ladies were going to have nightmares for years to come.... but at least we had managed to stop the actual nightmare, and stop others from being drawn in. In the real world, outcomes are never perfect, but if you can make things better to the best of your ability, you are doing better than most. Driving back to Beaver Valley we discussed the outcome. Sonny was good with it. We decided to tell the ladies about the pile up on Saturday morning, but conveniently omit the events of Saturday afternoon. Suffice to say that Bullwhips day's of terror were over, and The Evil Ones were all in hospital in various stages of disrepair and leaderless once again. I could hardly wait to get back to Dawn. I could tell Sonny was thinking the same about Sue.

EPILOG

Some years back I gave my mum a plant I had
found, when she was trying to build a garden on
next to no money. Looked pretty to me. She smiled,
gave me a hug, gave me a kiss, then told me we
better burn the thing. Puzzled, I asked why. She told
me it was Japanese knot weed, and I remember her
exact words: "David, this is an evil one. It is one of
the most invasive plants known to man. Once
planted it will take over, killing everything, even
capable of pushing through what you would think
were impenetrable barriers like concrete or asphalt.
Cut it down, and it comes back twice as strong."
I could only hope that I had cut down The Evil Ones
I met for the last time.

On the following pages you will find information that I hope you will find interesting.

This is my first work of fiction. Profits will be going to Cats Anonymous. I hope to write more works of fiction (practice they say makes perfect :-) and would appreciate your comments on my web site.

www.barrytuddenham.com

On my site you will find some exceptional contests and give a ways... I promise you a visit will be worth your while.

THE CEDAR WAXWING

Benjamin Franklin said "Beer is proof that God loves us and wants us to be happy." He also said "in wine, there is wisdom, in beer there is freedom, in water there is bacteria." Good old Ben..... a man after my own heart.

Some of the best people I know enjoy a drink...helps to make some of life's insanities bearable (anyone that thinks life is not crazy has not been paying attention). In the animal kingdom, it is cedar waxwings that often get intoxicated on fermenting berries sometimes falling out of the tree. Getting drunk can be the death of them, as they are easy targets when drunk on the ground, and while we all know driving while intoxicated is bad, flying while intoxicated is REALLY dangerous.

I am not used to seeing drunks stagger around our back yard(the neighbours may have seen me in that state a few times, but that is another story entirely) When I did about 12 years ago, I rushed to the rescue. The little cedar waxwing was easy to catch and cage. After a few days in a drunk cage with fresh fruit to flush out his system he was right as rain and eagerly rejoined his buddies when we released him. Cedar waxwings are very social birds. I don't know if it was the same flock, but they accepted him anyway. Not only are waxwings incredibly beautiful, they are fascinating to watch for their antics. Non-territorial, they flock together communicating amongst themselves in a complex mix of trills whistles and buzzes we do not understand. Often they can be seen passing a flower petal or leaf back and forth in some sort of game. The original flower children? If the flock is hungry and comes across a berry laden branch that is too fragile to hold more than one bird at a time, one will climb on while the others line up. The collector will then pass the berries down the line beak to beak so that everyone gets a meal. The waxwing is one of the most frugivorous birds in North America. That is not as rude as it sounds. Just means they are fruit eaters. Great word, isn't it?

Because waxwings rely so much on fruit, they are one of the last birds to nest, allowing them to take advantage of the late summer and fall crops. Once a couple have paired off for the summer, they are monogamous for that year. They both help build the nest and the female incubates about 5 eggs for a couple of weeks, with the male bringing her food and guarding over her from a perch higher than the nest. When the young are first hatched, the adults feed them insects for the first few days, and can catch insects while flying. They quickly switch the babies over to berries though. Adults can store a couple of dozen choke cherries in their crop (a pouch in the throat) and regurgitate them one by one for the babies. In another couple of weeks the young are ready to head off on their own. They will usually flock together with the young from other nearby families. If the first mating is successful, the adults may mate again, but the young will not mate until the following year at the earliest.

During the winter they rely heavily on

cedar berries, hence the first part of their name. The waxwing part comes from the red tips to the feathers, that look as if they have been dipped in sealing wax. They are indeed a beautiful bird, in looks and in temperament. Every spring I look forward to seeing them in the mountain ash, and toast them .

DAVID'S VIEWS ON THE TEN COMMANDMENTS.

Exodus 20:2-17 The 10 Commandments. One and Two are just plain funny to me.

One tells people they must have no other God. Seems to me that, conservatively, 95% of the people around me worship Mammon...the almighty buck. Often, the people going to church the most seem the worst in that regard. Right now we live in a time when greedy bastards are destroying the very environment we need to survive, and yet what issue dominates every election? The economy.

Two says God is a vengeful God wreaking vengeance on the children to the third and fourth generation of those that piss him off or do not keep his commandments. Doesn't say keep some of them some of the time. This guy is talking total commitment here. Have never known anyone that had kept them all.

I have known some really mean bastards that would use violence on a man's family to intimidate him.... but for three or four generations? That takes things to a whole new level. Does anyone really want to spend eternity with someone that thinks like that. REALLY? An eternity of that makes fire and brimstone sound like a summer resort. Think if I were faced with that, I would have to try and kill myself....but I don't think that is possible if you are 'enjoying' eternal life. Reminds me of Damion's joke about hell .

Commandments Three, Four and Ten? Maybe it is just the company I keep, but I don't know a single soul that has not broken at least one of those. Most of them break at least one of them every day.

Seven and Eight? Now those make sense to me. Seven says you should not commit adultery. When I was single, any married woman that was interested in doing the horizontal mambo, I was up for it, if you will pardon the pun.... but that was technically not adultery on my part. Was on hers. Way I figure it, they had their reasons and the only thing I held against them was the thing they wanted. Now that I am married, I don't indulge in adultery. Nothing to do with religious doctrine though. It was just too damn hard to find the right woman, so why destroy it? Betrayal in any form is a destructive beast. Best not to mess with it. Similarly, stealing from someone, commandment eight, is a really bad idea. I don't think you ever get to enjoy what you stole. Short term gain, long term loss ....

You'll notice I did not mention Five and Six. Five is that honour your father and mother thing that I already covered. So, that makes three out of the ten I can agree on. Six is you shall not murder. I can see where most people think that is a good thing, but I am afraid I think sometimes killing is called for. That conclusion changed me and the course of my life forever....but I don't think it changed me in a bad way. I sleep better than most at night.

Those are just my opinions. You do not have to agree with them. You can do as you please as long it does not hurt me or something or someone I care about . I would not judge me too harshly if I were you unless you have really taken a good look at your life. The vast majority of North Americans are so busy worshipping mammon that they don't bother to think about the atrocities being carried out constantly so that they can have cheap food on their tables. I do. They don't bother to think about the poor bastards slaving for a dollar a day so that they can have cheap goods. I do. There is good and bad in most of us. I like my mix. Anyone who thinks this is a fair world or that we don't all have our own brand of crazy has just not been paying attention. Might as well finish my little rant here with another bible quote. Matthew 7:1-3. "Judge not, less ye be judged."

Recipes

Soup.

The perfect vegetable soup for people not struck on the taste of veggies! This recipe calls for a lot of veggies that some people do not care for, but the spices tend to cover any strong taste. Fresh is best, but use frozen veggies if fresh not available.

1/2 cup chopped onion
2 carrots thinly sliced
2-4 potatoes in small cubes
1/2 cup chopped turnip
2 stalks of celery, thinly sliced
3/4 cups green beans, chopped
1 cup peas
1 can of beef broth
1 can of water.
Cook on medium heat for about 10 min. Then add:

28 oz can of chopped tomatoes
1 can tomato sauce.
2 cups of chopped spinach (or half package of frozen if no fresh available)
2 cups green cabbage, chopped fine
Tabasco sauce to taste (I like about 1/2 tsp. You can always add more in the bowl if you want it.)
1 tsp oregano
1 tsp basil
salt and pepper to taste
2 to 4 cups of water, depending on how thick you want it to be.
Bring to boil, then turn down and let simmer for an hour or so, stirring occasionally.

David's Favourite Bread Recipe

You may want to cut this recipe in half..... takes a lot of muscle to kneed this much dough. Makes about 6 loaves as is.

8 medium sized potatoes (save the water!)
6 tbsp of butter
3 packs of yeast
4 tbsp pf sugar
4 tbsp of salt
1 to 2 cups of cracked wheat
16 to 18 cups of strong bakers flour (add until dough no longer sticky)

If making full recipe, use a very large pot. Peel and cut up potatoes (smallish chunks) I use Yukon Gold, but sure others would work as well. Bring to boil in about 7 to 8 cups of water .Cook for about 15 minutes, and drain...BUT.
Save the water. Mash, and add the butter. Then put back in 6 cups of the potato water and stir until mashed potatoes are dissolved. Let cool until luke-warm (approx. 80 degrees) . Add yeast and let it start activating (approx 10 minutes) Add the salt and sugar. Add the cracked wheat. Keep adding flour until dough is no longer sticky....I usually find that to be about 16 cups, but depends on the flour.

For full recipe, need two large bowls. Cut dough in half, grease bowls put half in each, then turn over so top is lightly greased.

Let rise 1 hour or a little more. Take out of bowls, and divide into greased pans.

Let rise another hour

Cook in oven preheated to 375 degrees for about 45 minutes.

ENJOY!!

Shepherd's Pie

First, put on about 3.5 to 4 pounds of potatoes to boil, while you prepare the meat section.

1 tbsp butter
1tbsp olive oil
large onion, diced up
3 cloves of garlic
1 large carrot, finely chopped up
1 celery stalk, finely chopped up
Couple of squirts of tomato ketchup (tablespoon or two)
2 to 3 lbs of lean ground beef
2 to 3 tablespoons of Worcestershire sauce
1/2 cup of beef stock (real beef drippings are better than canned stuff if you have them left over from cooking a roast... just add boiling water to two or 3 tablespoons of drippings .... without the fat)
1 can of peas, drained
Celery salt
Salt and pepper

add the butter and oil to a large frying pan, place on medium heat. Saute the onions, carrot, celery and garlic for about 10 minutes or so. Season with celery salt. When veggies start to brown, add the ketchup. Then, add the beef and cooked until all brown (no pink meat showing) About 10 minutes or so. (Might want to drain the potatoes now if they are nicely cooked) Add the beef stock and the Worcestershire sauce (like the taste of this, so I use a little more....but it is strong stuff...don't overdo.) Salt and pepper to taste. Leave on low while you prepare the potatoes, stirring occasionally.

For the potato topping you need
3.5lbs to 4 lbs potatoes
4 tablespoons of butter
1 to 2 cups of very old cheddar, grated
Salt and pepper

Mash the drained potatoes, adding the butter, and salt and pepper to taste. Grate up the cheddar and mash in.

Put the meat mix in the bottom of a large pan. I use a spoon to put the potatoes completely over the top, covering the potatoes, then use a fork to smooth the potatoes over so that the layer is complete and even. Use the for tynes to leave groves in the top...will help it brown

Cook for about 20 minutes. I usually turn the broiler on for a few minutes to make the mashed potatoes nice and brown on top.

Date and Nut Loaf

1 cup of pecans, chopped
1 cup dates, chopped
2 tsp baking soda
1/2 tsp salt
2 to 3 tbsp of shortning
3/4 cup boiling water
2 eggs
1 tsp vanilla
1 cup of sugar
11/2 cups flour

Mix the pecans, dates, soda, salt, shortening in the boiling water. Set aside for half an hour.

Beat the eggs with a whisk, add the vanilla, sugar and flour and the previous mixture. Mix thoroughly.

Put in greased and floured pan

Bake at 350 for a little over 1 hour.

Home Made Dog Biscuits

As a member of the family, your dog should have healthy, tasty treats too!

11/2 cups whole wheat flour
1 cup all purpose flour
1 cup skim milk powder
1/3 cup melted beef or bacon fat if you have it. If not, use olive oil
1 egg
3/4 cup of water.

Combine flours, milk powder and melted fat (or oil)
Add the egg and water. Mix well.
On floured surface, with sprinkling of flour on top, roll out to approx. 1/2 inch thick, or a little less. Cut into desired shape, gather scraps into a ball, and repeat until all used.

Bake on un-greased sheets at 350 for about 45 minutes.

(OK I admit it. I have tasted them. Don't see the appeal, but my dogs love them!!)

EXAMPLES OF DAMION'S JOKES

A man gets on a plane to take a short 300 mile trip to the city. As he sits down, the seat belt automatically activates. Unfortunately, the belt is set to adjust to a size 36 waist, and he is a 42. The pain is excruciating. He reaches up to call the stewardess, but before he can reach the button, a door opens above him, and out falls a tray, a cup and a saucer, which all promptly fall on the floor. Immediately following, scalding hot coffee starts to pour out of the door, landing in his lap. Because of the belt, he cannot move out of the way, just sits there, roasting his nuts in tea. He reaches for the button again, but as he does, the plane starts to take off. Not a gentle take off, but rather a mad rush forward followed by an incredibly steep climb. The overhead doors all open, and the air is filled with flying suitcases and the like. He is knocked out by a particularly heavy one. When he awakes, his head pounding, his crotch still burning, he once more tries to call the stewardess.... but is interrupted by an announcement.:

"ladies and gentlemen. Welcome to the world's first fully automated non stop flight to Singapore! We will be landing in exactly 12 hours, 22 minutes, 14 seconds. There are absolutely no human staff on this flight. Everything will be done by machine. Your every need will be taken care of. We want to assure you that nothing can go wrong, go wrong,go wrong,go wrong,go wrong,go wrong,go wrong,go wrong,go wrong,go wrong,go wrong........."

Hitler is sitting in his bunker near the end of World War 11. He keeps receiving messages about defeats and humiliations, one on top of the other. His generals have all deserted him. Just then, a bomb lands on his bunker, almost deafening him, and showering him in dust.

"That's it! Enough is enough! They are starting to piss me off. No more Mr Nice Guy!!"

A piece of string walks into a bar in the wild west, and asks for a drink. The bartender looks at him and says "Hey. Ain't you a piece of string?" The string confirms his suspicion.

"We don't serve string here!" and with that he tosses the string out the swinging doors. The string is furious and rolls around in the dirt getting frayed and knotted. Then he stands up and goes back in and demands a drink.

"Ain't you the piece of string I just gave the bum's rush to?"

"No sir! I am a frayed knot."

Same bar. A dog limps in, gun belt around his middle, and announces to everyone in bar:

"I'm looking for the man who shot my paw."

A lady walks into the only general store in East Armpit, Alaska.

"Good morning" she announces cheerfully. "I'd like a pound of fresh raspberries please."

"I'm sorry madam. You must be new in town. You can't get fresh raspberries here, except in season. Come back in July."

Next week, she comes back in, with the same cheerful request.

"Sorry lady. You were in here last week. Don't you remember? We are the only store in town. I told you last week. You can't get fresh raspberries here, except in season. Come back in July."

Next week, same thing. Week after week, month after month.

The winters are long, and the man is finding this very hard to take.

Next time he sees her walk in he stops her before she can make her request.

"Lady. Before you ask me anything, I want to give you a quiz."

Oh, how nice. I love quizzes" she beams

"OK. This is a spelling quiz. Spell 'blue' as in blueberries. She spells it, no problem. B L U E

"You are doing great" She beams again. "spell 'straw', as in strawberries" S T A....no, no, S T R A W

"Lady, you are fantastic. Now the biggie. Spell 'fuck' as in raspberries."

"F U ..... just a minute. There ain't no fuck in raspberries...?"NOW you've got it lady....."

Information on Biker Gangs,
AKA 1%ers

Biker gangs. I'm sure most of you have had little to do with them. Sure most of you don't think about them much. Just as you have had little to do with terrorists or extremists. You don't think about them either unless they do something to make front page headlines. They stay in their world, you stay in yours. Really, you should think about them more. As the world evolves, and the gap between rich and poor becomes ever wider, they will become more prevalent. Thinking about such things could change...save...your life.

Motorcycle gangs came to prominence after the second world war. Perhaps the most famous being the Hells Angels. The name Hell's Angels was used by a squadron of the Flying Tigers during world war two. When it was taken over as a name for a motorcycle club, the apostrophe was missed out. Think a none too literate biker messed up....but they like to say the apostrophe was deliberately left out after a debate over just how many Hells there were. I am not going to argue with them. Not people I want to argue with.

In all wars, people learn to kill and maim for their country. The toughest of the tough are revered . Think about it. Who do you want guarding your back, someone that will try to talk some sense into the enemy, or someone that will do anything necessary without a qualm ? A few of those guys upon return will be hailed as heroes, and may be lucky enough to benefit from their heroism in battle when the war is over. The vast majority however come back to a world that has moved on without them Wives and girlfriends have gone, jobs have been taken by someone else, and nobody really cares about them. Indeed, most people are scared shitless of the really tough ones that come back many times tougher. Coming back from the hell of World war 11, lots of hardened vets were totally lost and joined motorcycle gangs, where they found people that accepted them. They had a family. The toughest of the tough drifted to groups like the Hells Angles, where their talents were admired.

A dramatic rise in motorcycle gangs and the one percent classification came about in 1947 after what are now referred to as the Hollister Riots. The American Motorcyclist Association sponsored a rally in the small town of Hollister, California. More bikers than expected turned up, and things became a little rowdy. Nothing serious, but the media sensationalized it, and made it sound as if the bikers had taken over the town. A few bikers got banged up from fights and spills off their bikes, but no town folk were injured. The media never mentioned that. 'Life' Magazine went so far as to print a staged photo of a guy, who looked nothing like an outlaw biker, on the back of a Harley, swigging beer and surrounded by empties. At the time, a quote attributed to the American Motorcyclist Association, said that 99% of motorcyclists were law abiding citizens, the remaining 1% were outlaws.

The rebellious misfit types loved that concept, and took it for their own. Hollister continued to host July 4th motorcycle rallies. The drunken behaviour was a problem, but the money was good. The sensationalized coverage increased their income. It also led to a huge increase in outlaw clubs.

The vast majority of outlaw clubs were not in the same league as the Hells Angels, not even close, even though to the general public all clubs were tarred with the same brush. Hell. These days you get accountants and lawyers buying expensive Harleys and trying to come off as bad bikers. Back in those days, that was not the case. They would have had the shit killed out of them by real bikers. The actual riding is not nearly as important as it used to be in many clubs.... making money is more important. Just like the rest of the world.

Ironically, a number of lawyers and a few accountants are now full patch members of clubs like the Angels... unlike the 1% of the professional class that try to look tough, these guys have actually become outlaws. They are welcome additions, and make a LOT of money, the lawyer members defending the club members in legal cases, the accountants helping them launder money. The major outlaw bike clubs are now big business. The Angels even brag that they have a number of judges on their payroll. There has never been a shortage of people ready to put on a show of piety, all the time worshipping mammon above all else.

Assuming the AMA calculation was correct, 99% of bikers are law abiding, even though a large percentage of that 99% like to act tough and instil fear, even if it is only on the weekend. Many of them are like my buddies back in the town I grew up in. Poor kids from poor families that the world looks down on and who are depended on for a source of cheap labour. Born to lose is an apt expression. Some decide not to take their fate lying down, and rebel. Most of them will drift back into mainstream society once those teenage years of raging hormones are over. But, a few will come under the wing of a real bad ass, a guy that does not have to *act* tough. There is good and bad in all of us. For some, the bad will win out over the good, and they will become more and more like their mentors. These are the ones that become the 1% ers AMA talked about. But AMA did not go far enough in their breakdown. Less than 1% of that 1% will become truly spectacular bad asses, drifting towards such organizations as the Bandidos, The Outlaws, the Pagan's, the Mongols, and the Hells Angels. The scum always rises. Indeed, these days if a motorcycle gang begins to gain some prominence, one of the top five clubs will usually move in and 'make them an offer they can't refuse' and they are what is called 'patched over' to the main club..or else.

Big money is to be made in drugs, prostitution, extortion, etc. Clubs like the ones mentioned above fight amongst themselves for the biggest share. Occasionally they will make the news as open warfare breaks out, but most of the time they like to pretend they are just fun loving guys having a bit of fun. Don't you believe it.

THE MOST DANGEROUS 1% ERS.

While we are talking about that 1 percent of 1 percent in the biker world, , there is a group far more deadly that often goes unnoticed. They are a group you are far more likely to run into. They affect your life far more than you know, and can do infinitely more damage. The irony is that although most of you would not be caught dead hanging out with the likes of the Hells Angels, many of you ache to be close to the others. It seems it is all part of the American Dream. In truth, I feel it is more aptly called a nightmare.

In North American society, 1% of the people own more than the bottom 90% of the population lumped together. That shock you? How about the fact that the top 1% of that 1% own almost all of that! It is a pyramid that has very few at it's apex. Indeed, just one family in the USA , the wealthiest family, owns almost as much as the bottom 40% own in total. True. Look it up..I'll give you a clue. You probably shop in their stores to save money. Bet you hardly ever give a thought to how they can provide goods so cheap. You should.

Now you probably do not live in that bottom 40%.... but think how someone that does feels. While you are at it, think how someone making a dollar a day in some country you probably never heard of feels. To them, the very poorest 1% in North America are immensely wealthy. Kind of puts things in perspective.

David, my main character in this novel grew up poor, right in that 40% I mention here. He got out. He's smart....but that is not the reason. He was incredibly lucky. There are a hell of a lot of smart people that never make it out. World wide, there are a hell of a lot of smart people that live in abject poverty. Most of them may not be educated, but trust me, most of them sure ain't dumb. They have the same percentages of smart and dumb , give or take, as we have here. But, they are all dirt poor. Can you really not understand why they rebel?

My mother has a saying " Big always wants more" Never in the history of the world have so few become so big at the expense of so many. I'd say something is going to blow sooner or later. I'd think about that if I were you. I'm just saying.

DAVID'S POLITICAL VIEWS
(Govt. of the people, by the people, for the people.)

Canada has a population of approximately 35 million people, of which approximately 25 million are eligible to vote. I suggest elimination of political parties..... the election of the right people for the job, not a party.

Starting at the local level, groups of between 100 to 200 people select one person from their group to represent them. As soon as more than 200 people are in the group, it splits into two groups. If a group drops below 100, it merges with the next closest group. This should be relatively easy to set up using a computer program. In return for participating in this process, each person gets a tax deduction receipt of say $2,000. Meetings are held monthly, on line if convenient.

The 100 people then get together once a month, once again, online if desired, and these people represent 10,000 voters. Each one of these groups of 100 selects one person to represent them.
Issues of importance to the country are discussed and suggested and sent in to the central committee. This 100 people receive an additional tax deduction receipt.

The one hundred individuals selected from 100 such groups get together, representing 1 million voters. There will be approximately 25 such groups across the nation. Each group selects one person to represent them. These people will be the people responsible for running the country. They will be paid for their services, as it will be a full time position. In addition, the best qualified experts on the issues of importance are sought out as needed to provide advice. Through use of the Internet, this does not have to be a static group elected every 4 years. The mix can be changing as required, and no one person maintains control.

Taxation would need to be remodelled. People earning below a living wage pay no tax. The ONLY deductions are for participation in the process as outlined here, and for charitable donations. Nothing else. The more you earn, the higher rate you pay. No loop holes. No lobbyists. No massive advertising campaigns to get elected.

Probably all sorts of flaws in this. But if an unpolitical person can think up a better way in a few hours, what could politically inclined people do if they put their minds to it?

DOBERMANS

One of the sweetest dogs you could ask for, and yet they have such a bad reputation. Part of that reputation is due to a few misconceptions.

Yes, Doberman's were bred to be a fearless companion. Indeed, they were developed as a breed by one Friedrich Dobermann, a tax collector in Germany in the 1890's . Tax collectors were as disliked then as they are today. But, I think Friedrich was also a very lonely man.... who wants a tax collector as a friend? So, he bred in a need to be close to humans, especially the owner. Dobermans by nature love to be around humans. It is said that if you get a Doberman puppy, you never have to worry about going to the bathroom alone! They follow you around, and hate to be locked out.

Many people believe that a Dobermans should be treated meanly, to make them good guard dogs. They are good guard dogs irregardless, and because they are so intelligent, treating them meanly just teaches them to be mean themselves for protection. Given socializing opportunities and the love they crave you will be blessed with one of the sweetest, most intelligent, loyal dogs you could ask for, with boundless energy and courage, and terrific strength, who gets along well with other people (unless they are acting aggressively towards the owners they adore), other dogs and children .

Many people think they look mean. Nothing could

be further from the truth. People crop their natural ears and tails in an attempt to make them look fearsome, but nature gave them floppy ears and a long tail that do not look anywhere near as frightening. I have a doberman. The meanest thing about him is that he likes to share the bed with me, and at 140 lbs, he tends to dominate the bed and steal most of my covers!

Dobermans were developed as a breed using a combination of Great Danes, German Pinschers, Greyhounds and Rottweillers.

This is a doberman of mine, called 'Harley' who is as sweet as could be at 140lbs, including his full tail and ears.
Every dog should have a 'tail' to tell, and ears to hear it!

BASICS OF HOLD'EM POKER
(and a few tips on how to play to win.)

Hold'em Poker is one of the most popular poker games these days. The no limit in the title just means that at any time, anyone can call 'all in' and put all his/her chips in the pot. Everyone must match the bet to stay in the game. Someone else with more chips can increase that bet, and everyone must then match that amount. No one has to put in more than they have on the table... indeed they are not allowed to add money from their pocket. In other words, if someone has $1,000 on the table and calls 'all in', and you only have $100, the most you bet and win or lose on is that $100. If there are just the two of you all in, if you win, you get your $100 back plus $100 of his. He gets $900 back. If he wins, he gets his $1,000 back plus your $100. 'All in' is often used as an intimidation tactic. It looks scary when someone with a big stack goes 'all in'.

Hold'em uses a rotating blind system to get the betting started. 'Blinds' are bets that must be placed before each round starts. The requirement to place blinds rotates to the left around the table so that everyone has to place them equally. At a table with nine players, each player will have to post 1 small blind and one big blind every nine hands. The small blind is half the size of the big blind. The big blind is equal to the minimum bet required at that particular table. A player posts the small blind. To his/her left, the next player posts the big blind. Then each person at the table, going in order to the left must either fold, call or raise. If you fold, you put nothing in and are out of that round. If you call, you match the bet placed before you. If you raise, you increase the amount bet before you, and from then on around the table everyone must either match your bet, increase it or fold. If the betting gets to the small blind and no one has placed a raise, the small blind can call, raise or fold. If he calls, he must put in the other half to make up to the table minimum. If he folds, he loses the half bet he was forced to make at the beginning. If no one has raised by the time the betting gets to the big blind, he can either call or raise. If he calls, his bet is already on the table, so he does not have to add anything. If he raises, he adds chips and everyone at the table must start all over again to fold, call or raise.

In hold'em, five cards (community cards) are dealt face up for all players to use. Each player makes the best had he/she can make with the best five cards they have out of the seven available: the two hole cards and any three of the five community cards. Betting can occur every time cards are exposed. Cards are exposed in three rounds: the flop, when three cards are laid down face up, the turn, when another card is laid down, and the river, when the final card is placed on the felt.

Especially in online games you see people going 'all in' on the two cards they have been dealt, without waiting for the flop. Usually, this is not a wise move. As Kenny Rogers said in "The Gambler':
You've got to know when to hold 'em
Know when to fold 'em
'Cause every hand's a winner
And every hand's a loser

Where that applies the most is right after the flop. A lot of people get all excited when they get dealt ace ace as their hole cards. They are nice cards to start with, but not magic winners. If you have two aces as hole cards and someone else has a four and a six off suit, and the flop comes down three five seven, that person has a straight and you only have a pair! Your odds on winning are very slim now. Even if another ace appears, unless the other card is one of those flop cards, thus giving you a full house, all you have is three of a kind and you are beaten by that straight. If you have a pair of aces in the hole, you definitely want to raise to stop making it worthwhile for that person with the four and six from staying in the game, but you really want to see that flop if you can. That is where reading people and watching how they bet becomes so important.

These are the approximate odds of making a particular hand, in the order of their importance:

One pair..............................1 to 1
Two pair...........................20 to 1
Three of a kind................ 45 to 1
Straight......................... 250 to 1
Flush .... 500 to 1
Full House .... 700 to 1
Four of a kind .... 4,000 to 1
Straight flush .... 70,000 to 1
Royal Flush............ 650,000 to 1

If you want to win more at poker, learn to watch for patterns in the way people bet. This can be done on line as well as in a live game. In a live game, reading tells becomes a very big factor.

Try to avoid the urge to go all in if you are dealt a couple of nice cards. For one thing, going all in scares away other bidders who you may make $$ off. For another, the odds are in your favour, but not enough to risk everything. Raise to get rid of the weak hands, but wait for the flop if you can.